BEAUTY'S HOUR

BEAUTY'S HOUR

A PHANTASY

BY

OLIVIA SHAKESPEAR

═══════════

Edited by ANNE MARGARET DANIEL

═══════════

VALANCOURT BOOKS

Originally serialized in *The Savoy*, August-September 1896
First Valancourt Books edition 2016

Published by Valancourt Books, Richmond, Virginia
Publisher & Editor: JAMES D. JENKINS
http://www.valancourtbooks.com

ISBN 978-1-943910-40-3
Also available as an electronic book.

Set in Dante MT

CONTENTS

FOREWORD

Two Writers: Shakespear and Yeats

Olivia Shakespear is best known today, if she is known at all, as a mistress and a mother. From 1895, her connection to William Butler Yeats – initially as his first lover, and then as his closest friend for many years – has been the reason modern readers know Shakespear's name. She is a principal subject of the memoir Yeats did not publish during his lifetime.[1] She was Yeats's best friend, theater companion, first reader for many poems, and sounding board and adviser – even after Yeats's marriage to her own brother's stepdaughter, thereby her niece, Georgie Hyde-Lees. Shakespear introduced Yeats to Ezra Pound, who married Shakespear's only child Dorothy, and took his make-it-new hammer to Yeats's increasingly Modern poetry.

Yeats, who in his writings loved forging and reshaping women he knew – or those, like Helen of Troy and Leda, he had encountered in books and then reimagined for himself – could or did not forge Shakespear. This makes her unique and tremendously important in Yeats's life and work: keen on balances and oppositions, points and counterpoints, comparisons and contrasts as he was, he found in Olivia someone who refused to do anything but stand alone and be constant in this, always reliable and steadfast. Biographers, particularly Roy Foster, have more recently begun to give Shakespear the place of prominence she deserves in Yeats's feminography. John Harwood, in the only biography of Shakespear to date (and still a biography principally in terms of Yeats and their connection), has carefully amassed the few surviving letters and documents of her life, written on her nearly-forgotten novels, and done justice to her influence on, particularly, the poems of The Wind Among the Reeds (1899) and upon The Shadowy Waters (1900).[2]

However, Shakespear remains too much an afterthought when one says "Yeats and women." I believe that Yeats's concep-

tion of women in his writing was shaped by Shakespear more
than by any other woman in his artistic life, including Maud
Gonne. It is notable and remarkable to find such companionship,
honesty, and – that cipher of a word – normalcy between Yeats
and a woman.[3]

For forty years, from the end of their first affair until her death,
only shortly before his, in October 1938, Olivia Shakespear was
the one soul who made no intense demands upon Yeats, expected
nothing in particular of him after the end of their first affair,
shared with him the grace of her company, conversation, and her
London homes – which were as important to Yeats the longtime
Londoner in some practical and necessary ways as Lady Augusta
Gregory's Coole Park was. Shakespear was the one person upon
whom Yeats could rely to give him her honest opinions on nearly
all matters without intrusions of self-interest, business, politics,
creative egotism, and the personal agendas that marked and
marred Yeats's relationships with all other women, and with
most men.

Such friends, indeed: in Yeats's own chronicling of female
friends, there's only one who is almost too precious for public
view in his poems and other writings, except for the memoir that
did not appear until 1972. Olivia is not left out because she didn't
matter, but because she mattered too much.

Olivia Shakespear first began to write fiction just before she
and Yeats met, in the early 1890s, when she was thirty and in a
passionless marriage (since 1885) to Henry Hope Shakespear, a
London solicitor fourteen years her senior. Of an upper-middle-
class family whose men had served in Queen Victoria's Little
Wars, most notably in India, Shakespear was also the cousin of
Yeats's good friend and fellow poet Lionel Johnson. She was an
extremely beautiful and intelligent woman; as Roy Foster puts it
succinctly, her marriage to the plain, cold Shakespear "is hard to
explain."[4]

Olivia Tucker was born on St. Patrick's Day, 1863, in a handsome house on the Isle of Wight that has since fallen down,
together with the crumbling chalk cliffs upon which it once stood.
She was a middle child; her sister Florence was seven years older,

and their brother, who rejoiced in the name Henry Tudor (and was mercifully called Harry), was three years her junior. She was close to both parents; her father, a retired officer, wrote letters to his young daughter showing an intimate relationship of equals. Tucker muses upon politics ("that poor Jew Dizzy") with Olivia, tells her secrets that he says he keeps from her mother Harriet, and in one lovely passage recounts his amusement at the engagement in 1881 of a wealthy family friend, Caroline Tremenheere, to a poor Irishman: "he is quite divine – Mother T. doats on him simply, & Caroline's love surpasses the love of ordinary women – he is so charming that when he departed for the East not only Mrs Trem & Cunningham & C. herself but even the foolish fat cook & housemaid all wept so they reported at least & Mama says that they were quite in earnest & serious & the drawback to all these charms of manner & character is that there are no Brass Farthings worth speaking of – & Carry is in consequence learning to stitch & sew & cook – Yes! Really – you may not believe it, but so her mother said – but only fancy – poor incapable Carry & she nursed in the lap of luxury ease idleness & oh! if he shd. turn out to be a Fenian in disguise or even a Land Leaguer & being Irish its quite impossible to know beforehand"[5]

When Olivia married, it was in her late twenties, and to a man far from being a Fenian or Land Leaguer – though he had travelled to, among many other places, Sligo to pursue his hobby as a landscape painter. Hope Shakespear, London lawyer, had enough of the touch of the artist to convince this beautiful woman to marry him. There is no evidence, though, that he was a sensitive and artistic soul. The honeymoon swiftly disabused Olivia of any such notion, and any romance ended at, or swiftly after, the altar, if we can believe Yeats's Memoir, quoting Olivia, on the point: "'[Hope had] ceased to pay court to me from the day of our marriage,' she had said."[6] Whatever the facts, one is unavoidable: nine months and some weeks after the wedding, Dorothy was born. The future Mrs. Ezra Pound was the couple's only child.

Unhappily, but comfortably, married, for a time Olivia contented herself with her daughter, an active London social life, writing – and writers. Her beloved cousin Lionel Johnson introduced her to his friends, and, when the circle had arisen, to The

Rhymers, that group of young men including Ernest Dowson, Richard Le Gallienne, Aubrey Beardsley, Symons, and Yeats. Richard Ellmann describes them beautifully as "futile, convinced young men" but had to admit that "The Rhymers furnished much of the talent for the *fin de siècle* reviews, the *Yellow Book* and the *Savoy.*" They loved Pater's prose, the pre-Raphaelite artists' painting and poetry, and as Yeats was immersed in his chief project of the early 1890s, his edition with Edwin Ellis of William Blake, he felt and showed the influence of this company. Johnson, already drinking in the manner that would kill him young, "made Yeats conscious of his own ignorance, telling him, 'I need ten years in the wilderness, you need ten years in a library,' and in 1893 presented him with a copy of the works of Plato and made him read it."[7] It's nice to know that we can thank Olivia Shakespear's cousin to some degree for Yeats's manifold shadows on the cave walls – his increasing neo-Platonic insistence, couched first in Celtic myths and then in other world legends and religions, that illusions and their lush counterparts, dreams, were more real than "reality."

In June of 1894 – after Yeats had finished his Plato – Shakespear's first novel, *Love on a Mortal Lease*, was published. It is nearly impossible today to find Shakespear's novels in libraries or through book dealers; when one can, the cheap, thick paper they were printed on practically turns to dust beneath one's fingers. The plot of *Love on a Mortal Lease* is not unlike those Shakespear would use later, nor unlike those of commonplace Victorian works. The heroine, Rachel Gwynne, has dead parents, as is the case from *Oliver Twist* (1837) through hundreds of other ensuing tripledeckers. Rachel is a novelist – most of Shakespear's heroines would be writers – in love with a military man many years her senior. After he refuses to marry her because he fears his mother will dislike Rachel and therefore disinherit him, Rachel becomes his mistress. Once the snobby old mother meets Rachel by happenstance in London, however, they immediately adore each other, and the Colonel may now safely marry Rachel – though she doesn't love him anymore, and he seems none too fond of her, either. They muddle along in unhappy matrimony until Rachel conveniently discovers (as we've known for a while) that the

Colonel has had another longtime mistress, a stupid society girl, throughout the course of their marriage, and even during their preceding affair. When the Colonel even more conveniently falls on his head and dies, Rachel is made a wealthy widow in her mid-twenties, free to marry a nice young writer who knows about, but forgives her, her former relationship. A happily wish-fulfilling story, perhaps, for a young woman writer in a bad marriage, and Rachel has some interesting ideas about her profession: speaking of clever girls who scribble, she hopes for the day that "the cleverness and the scribbling . . . fall from her, like a disguise, and she stands revealed in her true form – then she may never write another word, or she may write something immortal."[8]

Shakespear had finished her draft and had a publisher, Osgood and McIlvaine, lined up when Lionel Johnson invited her to a writers' event that April. The party was for *The Yellow Book*; the place, Hotel d'Italia, in Old Compton Street, London. Willie Yeats was at the supper party, and it was here that he and Shakespear first met. Arthur Waugh, Evelyn's father, went there with Yeats on public transportation, as he wrote the next day in a letter to Edmund Gosse "at Baker Street we were joined by W. B. Yeats. Have you met him? A tall sallow, black haired youth with the jaw of a monk, & a sort of catch in his voice – rather an interesting personality, tho he would talk about the theory of poetry inside a bus, which seriously alarmed two homely old ladies and scandalized a City man."[9] And here is the tall, sallow, black-haired youth's own account of first meeting Shakespear:

"At a literary dinner where there were some fifty or sixty guests I noticed opposite me, between celebrated novelists, a woman of great beauty. Her face had a perfectly Greek regularity, though her skin was a little darker than a Greek's would have been and her hair was very dark. She was exquisitely dressed with what seemed to me very old lace over her breast, and had the same sensitive look of distinction I had admired in Eva Gore-Booth. She was, it seemed, about my own age, but suggested to me an incomparable distinction. I was not introduced to her, but found that she was related to a member of the Rhymers' Club and had asked my name."[10] The passage needs no parsing.

Nor does Shakespear's reaction to him need deep investigation. She was beautiful when they met – what did Yeats look like? We've got Waugh's description that you've just read. And there is the cynic's view, as voiced by Violet Martin to Edith Somerville: "He is thinner than a lath – wears little paltry clothes wisped around his bones, and the prodigious and affected greenish tie. He is a little affected and knows it – He has a sense of humour and is a gentleman – hardly by birth I fancy – but by genius."[11] Martin, though always wickedly clever, might not be the best judge of male attractiveness. We have, after all, the photographs of that iconic 1890s face, the dark flowing hair, the deep eyes, the Byronic collars. And we also have the way George Moore described his friend in *Evelyn Innes*, a book published a few years later. Yeats wrote, rather proudly, to Augusta Gregory on the first of June 1898, getting the name of his character not quite right and with advice designed to cut into Moore's sales: "Get Moores Evelyn Innes from the library. I am 'Ulric Dean,' the musician." Two weeks later, he reported to Gregory that he was reading *Evelyn Innes* aloud to Maud Gonne.[12] And no wonder; here is Yeats as Ulick Dean: "He had one of those long Irish faces, all in a straight line, with flat, slightly hollow cheeks, and a long chin. It was clean shaven, and a heavy lock of black hair was always falling over his eyes. It was his eyes that gave its somber ecstatic character to his face. They were large, dark, deeply set, singularly shaped, and they seemed to smoulder like fires in caves, leaping and sinking out of the darkness. He was a tall, thin young man, and he wore a black jacket and a large, blue necktie, tied with the ends hanging loose over his coat . . . Ulick's teeth were almost the most beautiful she had ever seen, and . . . they shone like snow in his dark face."[13]

Olivia immediately asked her cousin to arrange a proper introduction to this handsome young man. She added a p.s. to the letter Johnson wrote to his friend, inviting Yeats to an afternoon at the comfortable, indeed elegant Shakespear home in Portchester Square, in mid-May: "I shall be so glad to see you."[14] Yeats remembered that meeting down to her words: "Presently the member of the Rhymers' Club introduced me to the lady I had seen between the two famous novelists, and a friendship I hope to keep till death began. In this book I cannot give her her real name – Diana Vernon [the name of the heroine of Sir Walter Scott's *Rob Roy* (1817)] sounds pleasantly in my ears and will suit her as well as any other. When I went to see her she said, 'So-and-so seemed disinclined to introduce us; after I saw your play [*The Land of Heart's Desire*, performed at the Avenue Theatre, now the Playhouse, in 1894] I made up my mind to write to you if [I] could not meet you otherwise.' She had a profound culture, a knowledge of French, English, and Italian literature, and seemed always at leisure. Her nature was gentle and contemplative, and she was content, it seems, to have no more of life than leisure and the talk of her friends. Her husband, whom I saw but once, was much older and seemed a little heavy, a little without life. As yet I did not know how utterly estranged they were. I told her of my love sorrow, indeed it was my obsession, never leaving by day or night."[15]

Though Shakespear remained anonymous as "Diana Vernon" in *The Man and the Masks*, Richard Ellmann's 1948 biography of Yeats (since Ellmann did not wish to make any possible trouble for Dorothy Shakespear Pound, dealing at the time with her husband's treason charges), there is no evidence that Yeats ever called her "Diana" to her face. Like Jonathan Swift, Yeats was always a great renamer of his women, giving them mythical aliases or the names of Sir Walter Scott's heroines, referring to them by Golden Dawn initials, and turning feminine Georgies into masculine Georges. However, Shakespear had a name, and names, that Yeats loved: the surname of his best beloved English playwright-poet, and the Christian name of one of Shakespeare's loveliest romantic heroines. It is perhaps inevitable that Willie should have told Olivia, finding her beautiful and open-minded, and a "woman of leisure" – a word that for Yeats has always the ring of liberty and grace to it – about his love sorrow and obsession. Not for nothing did George Yeats dub her husband "William Tell"[16] – he was a gutspiller from early youth. Shakespear knew about Maud Gonne, Yeats's "love sorrow," from the start – and much to her credit, and to the continuing power of her friendship with Yeats, she never pretended not to have.

On January 30, 1889, Gonne had arrived at the Yeats's door on Bedford Road for political discussion and, in the opinion of Lolly

Yeats, something else. Lolly wrote in her diary that evening: "Miss Gonne, the Dublin beauty (who is marching on to glory over the hearts of the Dublin youths), called today on Willie, of course, but also apparently on Papa. She is immensely tall and very stylish and well dressed in a careless way. She came in a hansom all the way from Belgravia and kept the hansom waiting while she was here. Lily noticed that she was in her slippers. She has a rich complexion and hazel eyes and is, I think, decidedly handsome. I could not see her well as her face was turned from me" – and toward Lolly's 23-year-old brother. Lolly recorded dryly the following day, "Willie dined at Miss Gonne's tonight."[17] The first time that Yeats wrote Maud Gonne's name, in a letter to John O'Leary some days later, he rather prophetically spelled it with one N.[18]

That afternoon at his father's house was the day, Yeats famously wrote, when "the troubling of my life began."[19] Both honest and foolish enough to pour out the story of his "love sorrow" to Shakespear in their first conversation, at least Yeats evidently never kept the truth of his feelings for Gonne from her.

Despite William Tell's self-indulgent honesty, Yeats and Shakespear began to write each other, to see each other at the Shakespears' home in the company of Johnson and others, and – most importantly – to share their work. The first surviving letter of their correspondence is her postscript to him on Johnson's letter – his first to her is a long letter, dated 6 August 1894, about *Beauty's Hour*. The letter is noted as property of Michael Yeats, as are nearly every one of Yeats's letters to her. One cannot doubt from this evidence that Shakespear returned Yeats's letters to him when he asked her to. Unfortunately, Olivia's correspondence for the years of their affair and its aftermath, 1895-1899, appears not to have survived. Of all her letters to Yeats, only a handful have been found and published – and we can tell from his replies to her that there were many more.

In this letter of August 1894, Yeats's language, as in so many other missives to her, is, for him, not only court-paying but flirtatious. The words he uses are intense and desiring, as he writes to criticize Shakespear's hero in *Beauty's Hour*, Gerald, as too undefined. Gerald is going to lose the girl, Yeats warns, exactly because he is *not* like Yeats: Gerald is "one of those vigerous [*sic*] fair haired boating or cricket playing young men, who are very positive, & what is called manly" but who are incapable of understanding a woman's character, heart, and soul. Yeats insists that men need "protection & care in those deeper things where [a woman is strong]." He speaks of longing to hear her read aloud, and, finally, refers to his letter – which he asked on the envelope to be forwarded to Shakespear (she and her husband were on holiday) – as doing what he is also doing, "pursuing you." As a postscript he adds the teaser "I have much to say" that he must perforce leave unsaid, as he must, allegedly, relinquish this manuscript now so as to be sure to catch the post. He makes her think, and keeps her wondering. Of course, he also praises her: the actress Florence Farr, who would soon be Olivia's collaborator in *The Bride of Hathor* and *The Shrine of the Golden Hawk*, is "very delighted with you." And Yeats is downright blissful that Shakespear likes his own stories; her liking of his stories is to him "a very great pleasure & the best of pleasures."[20]

Olivia shared, to some degree, Yeats's interest in visions and in the occult – interests that increased after her recognition that Yeats was so keen. That interest shows clearly in Dr. Trefusis's character in *Beauty's Hour*. Though he is styled as a serious scientist, Trefusis's library seems to contain only works of alchemy, Renaissance magic, mysticism masquerading sometimes as theology, and the occult. It is a library designed not only to rationalize the doctor's interest in Mary Gower's experiment in turning herself into Mary Hatherley, but to delight Shakespear's soon-to-be lover.

Yeats continued to write to Shakespear about her drafts. In 1895 he used Romantic, Platonic language to explain that fiction should not be "mere phantasies but the signatures – to use a medieval term – of things invisable & ideal," and told her how much he liked her subject matter and her literary style: "I no more complain of your writing of love, than I would complain of a portrait painter keeping to portraits ... I have never come upon any new work so full of a kind of tremulous delicasy, so full of a kind of fragile beauty as these books of yours however."[21] As Roy Foster rightly notes, he's engaging in "calculated flattery"[22] here, for clear reason – but Yeats is right about both her genuine and graceful treatment of love as a theme, and the fragile beauty of her work.

Shakespear and Yeats began planning an affair by mid-1895, if not before. They were serious about each other to the point of eloping – with Olivia leaving behind husband and child for him, as she would have had to under law at the time. However, when Yeats had returned to London from Ireland that May, he was quickly caught up both in the furore of the Oscar Wilde trials, and planning *The Savoy*. It was also a dreadful time for Yeats at home in Bedford Park, where he lived still: his mother remained in bed, his aunt in an asylum, his brother Jack was married and gone, his father depressed and unable to paint.[23]

When Yeats moved into Fountain Court with Symons, where they sublet a suite of rooms from Havelock Ellis, his affair with Shakespear took another baby step forward. Though he was writing much poetry at the time, it is too easy to forget that by 1891 Yeats was a published novelist. His autobiographical *John Sherman*, published in 1891 by T. Fisher Unwin under the pseudonym "Ganconagh" (an Irish fairy, Yeats explained), particularly influenced *Beauty's Hour*. *John Sherman* is a novel of humor, even elegance, and Yeats's depiction of Sligo – renamed Ballah – is memorable. Just as he was (no matter how he tried to deny or scoff at it) a born businessman, Yeats was also a born editor. His suggestions, some made in that first letter to Shakespear, color the characters of *Beauty's Hour*, their relationships, their interests; and *John Sherman* is clearly a book Shakespear has not only read, but studied. Its autobiographical nature must have made it fascinating to a woman falling in love with Yeats. She not only quotes directly from the novel in the climactic, concluding scene as Mary Hatherley and Gerald are parting for the last time, but uses Yeats's bluff sporting character William Howard in Gerald; his flirtatious and spoiled Margaret Leland in both Bella Wilfer and Mary Hatherley; and – chiefly – the calm, steady Mary Carton in Mary Gower. Sherman himself, the Yeats character, is the only one Shakespear doesn't touch.

Their initial connection as writers of fiction had given them an intellectual and artistic link, and now, living out of his family home in his own rooms, Yeats had a place to be alone in private with Shakespear. However, he was not *quite* alone there – Arthur Symons was too often at home working feverishly on plans for *The Savoy*, writing, or keeping Yeats awake at night with stories of the latest dancer or snake charmer or little Lolita who had infected his eye. And, with the idea of Maud Gonne still powerfully in his head and heart, Yeats could not commit to Olivia. He is so plainspoken about this in his *Memoirs*, in patches brutally so, as to seem entirely honest: Shakespear's "beauty, dark and still, had the nobility of defeated things, and how could it help but wring my heart? I took a fortnight to decide what I should do. I was poor and it would be a hard struggle if I asked her [to] come away, and perhaps after all I would but add my tragedy to hers, for she might return to that evil life. But, after all, if I could not get the woman I loved, it would be a comfort even but for a little while to devote myself to another. No doubt my excited senses had their share in the argument, but it was an unconscious one. At the end of the fortnight I asked her to leave home with me. She became very gay and joyous and a few days later praised me [for] what she thought my beautiful tact in giving at the moment but a brother's kiss. Doubtless at the moment I was exalted above the senses, and yet I do not [think] I knew any better way of kissing, for when on our first railway journey together – we were to spend the day at Kew – she gave me the long passionate kiss of love I was startled and a little shocked."[24]

Still more time had to pass. In order for the couple to meet "officially" at Fountain Court, Yeats arranged for Symons to be invited to the Shakespears,' and then Symons invited Olivia and Valentine Fox, her "sponsor" or chaperone for their affair – imagine a world in which affairs needed chaperones – to tea at Fountain Court in autumn of 1895. Symons then discreetly absented himself, leaving the moment to Shakespear, Yeats – and Fox. Yeats, with his mind on Maud, proceeded to go out and buy cake for tea and forgot his latchkey. Tea was delayed while a man more agile than Yeats "climbed along the roof and in at an attic window." After the ladies left, Yeats talked for three hours that night to an exhausted Symons, who had stayed out until midnight to give Yeats some space, not about Olivia and the afternoon, but about Maud.[25]

Almost immediately thereafter, as if she knew what was transpiring in London, Gonne began writing to Yeats more frequently than she had in months. No longer in France, where she and Lucien Millevoye had lost a son and separated for a time, Gonne had retreated to Dublin – and, back in Ireland, her mind turned to Yeats. In the Maples Hotel, Kildare Street, in November 1896, she wondered if he was thinking of her. Was he dreaming of her, she asked? For she was dreaming of him. And Maud, like young Laura Armstrong before her but far more surely, knew exactly what Yeats wanted to hear: just before midnight, Gonne has had a vision of him with her on Howth, that untamed headland surveying the entrance to Dublin port, every bit as magical to Yeats as to Joyce. "I saw you again and together we went down to the cliffs at Howth, but the sea birds were all asleep & it was dark & so cold, & the wind blew so horribly. I came back & quite woke up, but I knew you were still not far off."[26]

Gonne came to London to find him soon after, and following dinner wrote to Yeats from the Charing Cross Hotel a letter she timed at "one o'clock morning" on Nov. 14: "I was very glad to see you, but very sorry to see that you were still troubled & worried. All I would say is go on with the great work you are doing for Ireland by raising our literature. For the honour of our country, the world must recognize you one of the Great Poets of the century. Be true to yourself & let nothing interfere with your literary work. This is surely your first duty. Do not let your life be tied down by other lesser ones."[27] Gonne's insistence that Yeats work for Ireland, Irish literature, and his own poetry – and that it is his duty to do so, ending with that terse directive on the prospect of his life being tied down by lesser things – really makes it sound as if Yeats must have told Maud about Olivia, exactly as he had told Olivia about Maud. Gonne might not have wanted Yeats herself, but she never wanted anyone else to have him, either. Yeats was both dissuaded and encouraged in the idea of marriage, kept on the hook for many years thereafter – first by Gonne, and then by her daughter Iseult.

To make matters even worse at this particular moment, Shakespear's "sponsor" Valentine Fox advised that they not seek a divorce for Olivia, and subsequent marriage. An unnamed friend of Yeats's advised the same: as Yeats remembered, "both, people of the world, advised us to live together without more ado."[28] This neither Shakespear nor Yeats, far more nice middle-class folk than bohemian writers, were willing to do. Shakespear did ask her husband for a separation, however, at this point – at which, Yeats recalled, Hope Shakespear "was deeply distressed and became ill, and she gave up the project and said to me, 'It will be kinder to deceive him.' Our senses were engaged now, and though we spoke of parting it was but to declare it impossible."[29]

Roy Foster makes the point that Shakespear's "(and literary London's) claims on [Yeats] were reinforced by the great event of 11 January 1896, when the first number of *The Savoy* was published in London."[30] For forty years to come London and Shakespear, and to a dramatic initial degree in 1896, *The Savoy* and Shakespear, were always linked for Yeats. The two poems by Yeats, and the short story, in that first number of *The Savoy* are about love of women and its difficulties – a theme he would never have to seek for, or contrive, throughout his long life. *The Shadowy Horses* (later *He Bids his Beloved be at Peace)* and *The Travail of Passion* are both quite Shakespearean, in the sense of Olivia. Maud Gonne also had long waving masses of hair, but hers was red; Trinity don Louis Purser provided a still-memorable contemporary description of Gonne as "a great red-haired yahoo of a woman."[31] These are poems for, and of, Olivia: "Beloved, let your eyes half close, and your heart beat/Over my heart, and your hair fall about my breast/Drowning Love's lonely hour in deep twilight of rest/And hide their tossing manes and their tumultuous feet." "We will bend down and loosen our hair over you,/That it may drop faint perfume and be heavy with dew. . . ."[32]

Yeats's story in the January number of *The Savoy* is "The Binding of the Hair," starring Aodh and Dectira, who would serve again, later and with slight name changes, as avatars for Yeats and Shakespear. She is the beautiful young wife of an old, foolish man, and he the traveling bard, singer of songs, visiting her husband's great hall. Aodh dies in battle; his head, hanging from a bush by its own dark hair, sings a song to the queen about her long tumbling dark tresses (the poem "He Gives his Beloved Certain Rhymes"). This Orphic song is cut short when "a troop of crows, heavy like fragments of that sleep older than the world, swept out of the darkness, and, as they passed, smote those ecstatic lips with the points of their wings, and the head fell from the bush and rolled over at the feet of the queen."[33] The singer of songs has, literally, lost his head over cascades of long dim hair.

There was another great event for Yeats in early 1896, a very simple one that made loving a woman not an abstract and spirit-linked literary epic, but a physical possibility: he finally got a room of his own. To consummate an affair was, for two polite and discreet people, amazingly difficult even in the decadent decade dubbed the *fin de siècle*, and even with a roommate as *laissez-faire* about such matters as Arthur Symons. There was no going to hotels; there were servants round and about in every home and country house; and London was a remarkably small town. On the technical front, as John Harwood matter-of-factly and also humorously reminds us, women's clothing took much time and effort to remove and to put on, and condoms were woeful: "Oisin had never been required to unlace a corset in near-freezing tem-peratures, or wrestle with a nineteenth-century condom, and Yeats's knowledge of these subjects was much the same as Ois-in's."[34] Yeats sadly remembered their being constrained to meet for more than a year "at Dulwich Picture Gallery and in railway trains" when he and Shakespear wanted to be alone.[35] So, finally, when he could almost afford to, Yeats moved in February 1896 from his shared rooms in Fountain Court into No. 18 Woburn Buildings, his London address for years to come. At the time, it was a run-down street; when John Masefield went there in 1900 he found "a kind of blackguard beauty about Woburn Buildings at night" and heard that "Yeats was known as 'the toff what lives in the Buildings.' He was said to be the only man in the street who ever received letters."[36]

Yeats furnished the rooms from bits and pieces bought and borrowed from Arthur Symons, including a table, a bolster, "7 pieces of tapestry canvas" "2 pieces of plushette" "2 blankets" and a fender and fire-irons – total value of everything, approximately three pounds.[37] Augusta Gregory found the "sitting room . . . very nice – large & low – looking on a raised flagged pavement where no traffic can come" but Yeats's bedroom, in the back, "very small

& draughty looks out on St Pancras Church with its caryatides & trees – . . . I wish poor W. cd be a little better waited on – his room had not yet been done up." Gregory was mistaken; the room had been done up, for Yeats had occupied it for a year by the time she wrote this letter. She was particularly bothered by the "remains of breakfast (cooked by himself) still there" – in the bedroom, that is; Yeats had no kitchen.[38]

The course of their affair, as briefly told by Yeats, is kind and sad and moving and, in the end, full of pain and also of beauty:[39]

> I took my present rooms at Woburn Buildings and furnished them very meagerly with such cheap furniture as I could throw away without regret as I became more prosperous. She came with me to make every purchase, and I remember an embarrassed conversation in the presence of some Tottenham Court [Road] shop man upon the width of the bed – every inch increased the expense.
>
> At last she came to me in I think January of my thirtieth [thirty-first, actually] year, and I was impotent from nervous excitement. The next day we met at the British Museum – we were studying together – and I wondered that there seemed no change in me or in her. A week later she came to me again, and my nervous excitement was so painful that it seemed best but to sit over our tea and talk. I do not think we kissed each other except at the moment of her leaving. She understood instead of, as another would, changing liking for dislike – was only troubled by my trouble. My nervousness did not return again and we had many days of happiness. It will always be a grief to me that I could not give the love that was her beauty's right, but she was too near my soul, too salutary and wholesome to my inmost being."

Friday was their usual meeting day, that late winter and early spring.[40] But Maud was firmly back in the picture – if ever she was gone – even as Yeats's affair with Shakespear began. That January she was, though not directly and couching it in terms of poetic and national duty, inviting him to join her abroad, and intimating that it was his own idea to do so: "Your idea of working in France is very good for an Irish Poet it would not be good to live always in London."[41] When word clearly reached her in Dublin of someone new in Yeats's life, in May 1896, Maud's letter to him is a masterpiece of manipulation and careful, allusive craftsmanship. As he was preparing to leave for Ireland for the summer, Maud reported as the latest local gossip "an interesting piece of news going about Dublin, taken I believe from some London papers ... that you have lately married a widow! At first I thought this could not be as having seen you in London [that spring past, as she was en route from Paris to Dublin] I thought we were sufficiently friends for you to have told me, but on reflection this is absurd as marriage after all is only a little detail in life (a foolish one generally I think, as one would have to spend so much energy & time in loosening a chain one had forged). So it is quite possible you are married & didn't think it important enough to talk to me about. Well if you are, I won't congratulate you, or even condole, as I hope it will make no difference in your life or work or character."[42] The widow in question was Rose Caroline Buddicom, who married Walter Baldwyn Yates, a London barrister, in 1896.

Yeats swiftly sent Maud *The Savoy* – tellingly, not the January number, with those poems and that story, and not the August and September issues, containing *Beauty's Hour*, but only the July issue, with his first article on William Blake and the poem *O'Sullivan Rua to Mary Lavell*. Gonne replied from Dublin to Yeats in Sligo, late in the summer, to compliment him on the Blake article without mentioning the love poem, but to say, specifically, that she wanted to see the earlier numbers of *The Savoy*: I "look forward greatly to reading your wild dreamy stories. I would like much to see you & have some long talks on many subjects, but I cannot come to the west. I would have loved to have spent a week in Sligo while you were there we would have tried if the fairies would have been good to us" – and oh yes, one more thing: "I shall hope to see you in Paris in the winter."[43] Before Christmas 1896, go to Paris he did indeed, in his own words following "the old lure," because Maud had called.[44]

From springtime until the end of 1896, Yeats and Shakespear had scarcely seen each other. Olivia had been writing; her novel *The False Laurel* appeared in June of 1896. Dedicated to Lionel Johnson, it is the story of a girl who wants to be a writer. However, she has the misfortune to marry an intense young poet who proves to be the real literary genius, and so she goes mad, destroys her own writings, and commits suicide. The young poet survives all with flying colors, and finds a nice girl in the end. Here's his concluding moment – just listen to Olivia's language, filled with Yeats's words, and also full of longing: the young poet has reached "not perhaps the land of his heart's desire, for which he had once set sail so confidently; but some island in still waters, where it was enough that the sun shone, and there was peace."[45]

But Yeats had headed off to his island in cold Atlantic waters, and with debatable sunshine, by the time *The False Laurel* appeared. Only a few months after he and Shakespear had begun making love in his rooms at the start of the year, Yeats left for Ireland with Symons for the summer, and ended up staying there for the rest of 1896. He met Augusta Gregory that summer – having been invited, he told John O'Leary proudly in June 1897, to stay at "Coombe, Galway"[46] – and began a very different sort of relationship with her. Symons liked Gregory at first, and was flattered by her "kind invitation" to come to Coole in the summer of 1899 with Yeats; he turned down the invitation because his proofs for *The Symbolist Movement in Literature* had just arrived.[47] Soon, though, Symons couldn't stand Gregory; by 1912, according to John Butler Yeats, he had dubbed her La Strega – the witch – "and moans at the mention of her."[48] Other friends of Yeats's agreed. Robert Bridges, in 1898, worried that "Yeats will go to the bad I am afraid. With his old woman who lives on the bog near Tuam."[49] Yeats's old woman was 44 when they met; we have a strange idea of Lady Gregory as perpetually sixty-something and overly regal, a sort of budget Queen Victoria, but perhaps this is because Yeats has handed her to us this way. Their meeting, while not nearly as devastating to Yeats's relationship with Shakespear as his connection to Gonne, certainly did not help. Gregory occupied his time and, from the beginning, he was enchanted by her house. Richard Ellmann's laconic comment, containing multitudes, upon Yeats's immediate enthusiasm that summer for Gregory and her work collecting local legends sums up much: "Never had Yeats been a more enthusiastic supporter of the peasantry."[50]

When Yeats finally did return to London and to Shakespear, in

January 1897, having scarcely seen her since May of 1896, Maud Gonne kept him on the line from Paris, writing to him immediately and often, flatteringly, persuasively, with promise. "[Maud] certainly had no idea of the mischief she was doing" to his relationship with Shakespear, Yeats stated later with amazing obtuseness, or calculated ignorance.[51] He couldn't daub it further: when Shakespear came to his rooms early in 1897, "instead of reading much love poetry, as was my way to bring the right mood round, I wrote letters. My friend found my mood did not answer hers and burst into tears. 'There is someone else in your heart,' she said. It was the breaking between us for many years."[52]

This is how Yeats recalled the end of the affair in his *Memoirs*. There is also the retrospective of his poetry, stranger and truer always for Yeats than those shifty, self-creating, often self-justifying, and sometimes revisionist *Memoirs* and *Autobiographies*. "Aodh to Dectora," also called "The Lover Mourns for the Loss of Love," first published in May 1898, and collected in *The Wind Among The Reeds* (1899), is an intensely autobiographical poem of Olivia and Willie – and the addressee is Maud.

> Pale brow, still hands, dim hair,
> I had a beautiful friend,
> And dreamed that the old despair
> Might fade in love in the end:
> She looked in my heart one day,
> And saw your image was there,
> She has gone weeping away.

Olivia's pale brow, leisurely hands, and long dim hair make her beautiful, but the most important word is friend. In his heart she has seen not a real woman, but the image Yeats recognizes he has set up there. As to how far away Shakespear went, how long her weeping lasted, and what constitutes many years: I suspect Yeats of self-indulgent drama on this part, and believe that Shakespear recovered fairly quickly from the end of their affair, perhaps engaging in another, and restored their friendship sooner than has been believed through her own choice. Ellmann, who clearly appreciated the "Diana Vernon" he came to know through George Yeats and the papers he was allowed to examine, is not kind to Yeats on the course of his first love affair, but he is not as unkind as Yeats, rueful and regretting, is to himself: "So much a part of him did his theories of unsuccessful action and unsatisfied love become that in 1895 and 1896, when a beautiful married woman fell in love with him, he spent the first year in idealized chastity, meeting her only in museums and railway carriages; and then, when they finally went to bed together, he kept expecting love to end until finally it did, and he returned to his former hopeless adoration of Maud Gonne and to his twilit state between chastity and unchastity. He was too ardent, underneath all his theorizing and idealizing, to be happy in this state, and so his poems are full of vague sorrow."[53] There's nothing vague at all about the sorrow in *The Lover Mourns for the Loss of Love*.

Yeats was a reactive person. It seems very probable to me that he turned back to Olivia's calm, attractive company after hearing from Maud, in December 1898, about her life and children with Millevoye. Olivia had not been weeping over him, or at least not only weeping over him, in 1897 and 1898; she had been working on a new novel, *Rupert Armstrong*. Published in January of 1899, and dedicated to the woman who had "chaperoned" her affair with Yeats, Valentine Fox, it is – finally – not a story about writers. It is, however, about artists. The patriarch and title character of the novel is a famous painter who Deirdre Toomey has argued, gracefully and most convincingly, is based upon John Millais – and the novel in places certainly tracks the story of Effie Ruskin, later Millais. That Rupert is also a portrait painter may have a touch of John Butler Yeats, too. Yet again, the heroine of the novel is a lovely young woman thwarted in her creative capacities by marriage to an old man; yet again, she is freed from this match and rewarded with a handsome young kindred spirit. Art does not always imitate life; often, it improves upon life. What didn't happen for Shakespear in her life could happen for her heroines in her novels.

While Shakespear was writing this book, Yeats was grappling with his play that is in many ways a tale of his time with Shakespear – *The Shadowy Waters* – and completing his collection of poems reflecting the best of the 1890s for him, namely Sligo and Shakespear – *The Wind Among the Reeds*. Though critics agree about the presence of Shakespear in these two volumes, biographers are variable as to just when Shakespear and Yeats reconnected as friends, and when, or even if, the two ever resumed a physical connection. Does the latter matter? Perhaps not, but it is more dreamy, and also more realistic, to believe that they did than that they didn't. Richard Ellmann, far closer to the time and to still-living people like George who would have known, speaks without doubt: Olivia broke off the affair in 1897 when she realized Yeats was still obsessed with Maud, but they "resumed it later, more casually, and remained good friends for life."[54] Roy Foster doubts: "Sundered as lovers, it is possible that a sexual relationship had been restored at some point; in any case, they were [by 1910] firmly reunited as friends."[55]

Yeats and Shakespear were far more in touch, and more intimately, from much sooner than anyone has quite been willing to say. In 1901, he was in torment over his autobiographical novel, *The Speckled Bird*, with its heroine originally named Olive. Yeats referred to the time from April 1900 to February 1901 as the "worst part of life. Both in regard to women matters & other things."[56] When he sat down at Coole Park in 1910 to do horoscopes and astrological calculations, Deirdre Toomey has shown that he devoted an immense amount of time and energy to details from Olivia's life.[57] But 1910 is far too late a date for their reconciliation. As soon as June 1897, bare months after their breakup, Yeats was already back in touch with Olivia, signing for her, on Bloomsday, a copy of *The Tables of the Law and The Adoration of the Magi*. (When this book sold in 1940 at Parke Bernet, in New York, its pages were uncut.)[58] Warwick Gould once mourned the absence of any signed copy of *The Wind Among Reeds* or *The Shadowy Waters*, "absences surely due to the estrangement of Yeats from Olivia Shakespear, and to the presence in both texts of an 'Olivia Shakespear' figure."[59] On December 19, 1900, Yeats did indeed inscribe a copy of *The Shadowy Waters*, in intimate words unique for him to use and absent his usual signing of his name, to "Olivia Shakespear from the writer." It is in private hands in New York.[60]

By 1900, Yeats and Shakespear were in regular communication, seeing each other alone and among friends, and sharing theater evenings. When Shakespear's mother died in May, only months after Susan Yeats's death, Yeats wrote movingly and from his heart to Olivia: "My dear Friend: I need not tell you how profoundly I sympathize with you in your sorrow. At such times there is little more that one can say, for those great sorrows are beyond any comfort that is in words. Of one thing and only one can I think be sure. It is very well with the dead & better than with the living. . . . The Irish poor hardly think of a mothers death as dividing her very far from her children & I have heard them say that when a mother dies all things go better with her children for she has gone where she can serve them better than she can here. That may endeed be the very truth."[61]

Olivia kept working, and soon began to write book reviews for a local monthly called the *Kensington*. Here's what she had to say, tartly and alliteratively, about a tome entitled *The Love Letters of an Englishwoman*, in early 1901: "The author of these letters is a sentimentalist and a prig; her effusions lack distinction, both of matter and of manner, they are pretentious, precious and prolix and at their best remind one of Mrs Browning at her worst." It is quite convivial and friendly that the June issue of *Kensington* carries a nice little contribution on a Celtic topic near to his heart, *The Fool of Faery*, by one W. B. Yeats.[62]

Their circles kept crossing, or, to be Yeatsian, their gyres kept running on, intersecting. Shakespear and Yeats's friend (and former lover) Florence Farr wrote two plays, *The Beloved of Hathor* and *The Shrine of the Golden Hawk*, and they were put on in London in 1902. Yeats went, and commented a little too circumspectly to Frank Fay only on their "decorative scenery" and their being "fairly well written." Well written indeed: well written enough for *The Shrine of the Golden Hawk* to be selected as the preview for Yeats's own *The Shadowy Waters* when it was finally produced in 1905. The *Times* reviewer, thinking the authoress of the former play must be Irish too, commended "O. Shakespear" as "a sort of present-day Swan of the Liffey." The reviewer also complained that *The Shadowy Waters* was "rather monotonous," and claimed that "only by a [mostly] heroic effort did I prevent myself from falling into as sublime a slumber as that which he dreamed for a blessing to the race."[63]

The Devotees (1904), Shakespeare's next book, is a rather creepy novel quite similar to that creepiest of Victorian novels, W.M. Thackeray's *Henry Esmond* (1852). The object of the central character Tony Atherton's devotion is his mother, the lovely, light-headed, loose Louise. Louise sleeps with many men while Tony goes to Oxford, where he marries one of his mother's former lover's daughters. Mamma is a cocaine addict, a pothead, and an abuser of morphine, but this does not stop her from marrying a nice young man her son's age in the end. Reviewers were uniformly horrified and took moral offense. Ezra Pound liked it and recommended it to friends, though with the caveat that the novel "is not nearly so enjoyable as she is."[64]

Yeats loved *The Devotees*, and found it, a bit perplexingly, a work of realism. He wrote warmly, passionately, to Shakespear from Coole that summer: "My dear ... the novel is a delight. I am only about two thirds through – I have got to Tonys discovery of his mothers drug taking – I cannot go quicker as my eyes are very bad indeed. It is much the best thing you have done. I know all the people intimately and I find all true & not the less charming & that is a rare thing ... I wonder at the skill with which you make one feal the passage of Time & at the same time make the change gradual like time itself. ...You must have been a young man & gone to school in Babylon or Alexandria. Perhaps you played with a pegtop somewhere in the hanging gardens." Upon finishing the book he found that the "whole book had a beautiful wisdom & sanity & gentleness," much like its author. Yeats also remarked how much he would be looking forward to Shakespear reading aloud her new work to him – as usual, it seems – when he returned to London.[65]

An account of an American interview with Yeats in 1904 has, perhaps, the loveliest and most secret moment of their renewed relationship, showing he is thinking of her. "Dim hair" – as already seen in "Aodh to Dectira" – is throughout the *Wind Among the Reeds*, Yeats's Sligo-and-Shakespear volume. The "long dim hair" of Bridget the bride, spliced in with the "passion-dimmed eyes and long heavy hair / That was shaken out over my breast," and the "dim heavy hair" of – very appropriately – "The Lover Asks Forgiveness because of his Many Moods" – all refer to Olivia. The only word in the *Wind Among the Reeds* Yeats uses as often as "hair" is "dim." Here's what the American interviewer, Ashton Stevens, asked him in 1904: Stevens wanted to know if Yeats was a decadent, and Yeats refused the category "good-humoredly." Then Stevens said, "One of your critics ascribes your decadence to your insistence on the hair in describing women – 'dim heavy hair' and such phrases." "'I think I know the one you mean,' Yeats smiled. 'And he did describe a mood in my work that is passed, whether for good or evil – I sometimes think for evil; for I can no longer produce in myself that mood of pure contemplation of beauty. . . .'"[66] Yeats was smiling, remembering whose beauty he'd been contemplating during the writing of those particular poems, and wishing, as he repeatedly does when speaking of Shakespear in his *Memoir*, that the mood had not passed.

In 1903, Maud Gonne converted to Catholicism, married (disastrously) Major John MacBride, and promptly became pregnant with his child. A second affair between Yeats and Shakespear that began, according to George Yeats, in 1903 – or even before – ended, I believe, when two things came to pass: Dorothy Shakespear left her home to marry the poet she loved, Ezra Pound, in 1914; and Maud Gonne was freed from the fact of John MacBride (though not her Catholicism) by MacBride's execution in 1916.

Critics and biographers of Yeats have tended to skip over Shakespear from early 1897 until 1910 or so, when she and Yeats were both in their fifties, and they had clearly, and publicly, reestablished a connection as friends. Even then, the focus of attention is not on Shakespear, but on Pound. A closer look shows that the focus of attention of both poets themselves, during this later time, was upon Shakespear. She shaped the lives of both Yeats and Pound in profound ways. Among the people Yeats met at Olivia's home, still in Kensington but now in Brunswick Gardens, and where he went regularly by 1910 when he wasn't out at the theater or at museums with her, were Pound, a 25-year-old American poet bent on making his acquaintance; Olivia's new sister-in-law, Nelly Hyde-Lees; and Nelly's two children from her first marriage, Harold, 20, and Georgie, 18.[67] Dorothy Shakespear and Georgie Hyde-Lees were best friends, and they would both marry the poets into whose company Olivia brought them.

Shakespear had a dramatic effect upon Pound; on meeting

her in early 1909 he reported to his mother that "a certain Mrs. Shakespeare ... is undoubtedly the most charming woman in London."[68] However, Olivia and Hope Shakespear both disapproved of Ezra's courtship of Dorothy, and she told him in the summer of 1910 that he was no longer welcome in their home – after Dorothy was already in love with him, and after he had already established his relationship with Yeats. Olivia relented, but slowly: the reasons why are speculative, apart from Pound's sad financial state, but I wonder if, even subconsciously, Olivia resented her daughter's offer of marriage from her poet, when from Yeats she herself had the same.

At first Pound and Yeats settled comfortably for each other's company instead – they lived together intermittently in Sussex, at Stone Cottage, during the winters of 1913 to 1915, with Pound famously, or perhaps infamously, serving as Yeats's secretary and editor. Yeats took Shakespear, whose brother had a cottage close by at Coleman's Hatch,[69] with him to check out the cottage before renting it.[70] Interestingly, Shakespear offered to Pound, after he and Dorothy were finally engaged in early 1914, a flat at 5 Holland Place Chambers, not far – but far enough – from the Shakespears' home, with a great main room shaped like a pentagram. Olivia's name was on the lease as its legal tenant, and when she had initially taken the space, and how long she had maintained it, are not certain. Apparently, she continued to pay the rent on these rooms of her own while Pound languished there and waited to marry her daughter.[71]

When Pound and Dorothy married, after their up-and-down, hot-and-cold six-year courtship, in April 1914 they spent their honeymoon at Stone Cottage (Yeats wasn't there), and then returned to live with Yeats for parts of the next two winters. Yeats wrote to Mabel Beardsley: "Pound has a charming young wife who looks as if her face was made out of Dresden china. I look at her in perpetual wonder. It is so hard to beleive she is real; & yet she spends all her daylight hours drawing the most monstrous cubist pictures."[72] Soon Olivia was raising her grandson Omar Pound, a rather ironic turn: having stayed with Hope Shakespear chiefly to maintain her place as Dorothy's mother, Olivia watched as Dorothy got to marry her poet – and as Georgie Hyde-Lees mar-

ried hers, too – while Olivia remained friend to all, and in loco
parentis to small Omar, whose stories of her, many decades later,
were told with immense love and admiration.[73]

What had become of Maud Gonne, while Yeats and Shakespear and, increasingly, the new additions to the Shakespear
family, the Hyde-Lees children, spent much time together in
1914 and 1915? Married to MacBride in 1903, mother of his son
in 1904, Maud had separated from him in 1905, but neither she
nor Yeats regarded her as a single woman thereafter until she
was widowed in 1916. After MacBride was executed, Yeats went
swiftly to France to console Maud, where he proposed yet again
to her – and then undertook an increasing obsession with Iseult.
After this came to pass, it's an unprovable, but most likely, sup-
position that Olivia ended her second affair with Yeats, and saw
him more or less safely to Georgie. The last moving moment
together between them, apart from the letters that continue
until her death, was at the end of 1914, and occurred in the same
manner and sort of space as their initial meetings at the Dulwich
Picture Gallery. Yeats wrote in his diary in December about a trip
he and Olivia took to the Sussex coast together: "at Rottingdean
two days ago Olivia & I were looking at the Burne Jones Window.
She was gazing at the Raphael window on the right. Presently she
said 'Don't think me a fool. It is the colour. It is like a sword. It has
carried me back twenty years.' When I looked at her she was in
tears."[74]

* * *

Yeats's marriage and the writing of *A Vision* (1925) inevitably
limited their friendship for a time. However, from the late 1920s
until her death Shakespear was Yeats's most casual and most intimate correspondent. Those things rarely coincide. To read Yeats
writing to her, and very occasionally a surviving letter of hers in
reply, is to see a side of Yeats that, both literally and literarily, no
one else did. A drawing he finds at Coole in 1926, of "two charming young persons in the full stream of their Saphoistic enthusiasm," got into Yeats's dreams, he tells her delightedly, "and made
a great racket there." Come and live in Rapallo, Yeats encourages

Shakespear late in 1928: "if one had not to take exercise life would
be perfect." From Rapallo, he complains that Ezra and Dorothy
have asked James Joyce to stay: "If he comes I shall have to use
the utmost ingenuity to hide the fact that I have never finished
Ulysses."[75] He always sent her drafts of poems – after she received
"Leda and the Swan," which Yeats referred to as a "lullaby," Olivia
shot back: "My dear Willy, your lullaby, though very beautiful, is
extremely unsuitable for the young! Leda seems to have a pecu-
liar charm for you – personally, I'm so terrified of swans that the
idea horrifies me."[76]

He begged for her advice and approval on the *Crazy Jane*
poems, both of which she honestly granted. He hand-delivered
copies of his books to her in 1933: "My copies only came on
Monday. I decided to bring you your copy out of sheer laziness."
In April 1936 he insisted that illness had at last made him "com-
paratively thin and elegant" once more, a reminder of his look in
1896. He asked his sister Lily to help out in embroidering presents
for Olivia: "I want to give Mrs. Shakespear a present of a table
centre and I have asked Sturge Moore to design it." He didn't
want tulips on it, as tulips have been "spoilt for us by Liberty."
Shakespear returns from a vacation to the country in 1917, and he
thinks about her skin: "I wonder if you are sunburned." Since he
was a little boy, Yeats had loved creatures: he kept beetles in his
pockets; one of his earliest letters features a rather good sketch
of a newt; he treated his cats like friends. When Olivia sent him in
1921 a nest of singing canaries, he was delighted, even obsessed,
with them. He wrote to her from Thoor Ballylee, asking for
appropriate nesting material as the number of birds grew, and
she shipped it to him from London. In no time there were four
nests of canaries to go along with the local birds in the tower's
battlements: "I have suggested a pie but George won't hear of
it."[77] As Yeats wrote "Sailing to Byzantium" and "Byzantium,"
the thought of those tiny, happy, singing golden birds from Olivia
was in his mind.

Upon learning of Shakespear's sudden death from a heart
attack, in October 1938, Yeats had this reaction: "For more than
forty years she has been the centre of my life in London and
during all that time we have never had a quarrel, sadness some-

times but never a difference. When I first met her she was in her late twenties but in looks a lovely young girl. When she died she was a lovely old woman. . . . She was not more lovely than distinguished – no matter what happened she never lost her solitude. She was Lionel Johnson's cousin and felt and thought as he did. For the moment I cannot bear the thought of London. I will find her memory everywhere."[78] Solitude is a strange word to use as a compliment – but Yeats wrote, decades before, to another friend that solitude was what he longed for most: "Solitude having no tongue in her head is never a bore. She never demands of us sympathies we have not. She never makes the near war on the distant."[79]

* * *

In his *Dramatis Personae 1896-1902*, Yeats says of himself, "A romantic, when romanticism was in its final extravagance, I thought one woman, whether wife, mistress, or incitement to platonic love, enough for a life-time. . . ."[80] Disingenuous, as much of Yeats's and indeed most autobiographies likely are, but his definition of romantic permits some sweeping prospects. For starters, Yeats's infamous insistence that his generation, and specifically he, was the last of the romantics. This let Yeats twin himself with not only the young romantics – particularly Shelley and Keats, but Byron is increasingly important as Yeats grows older – but also culminate what Coleridge and Wordsworth began in 1798 with *Lyrical Ballads*. Most importantly, Yeats permits himself to pick up the mantle of his favorite poet of the Romantic period, Blake, for what he decrees to be a final wearing. That one woman, if there was one for Yeats, was not Olivia Shakespear. However, she stood above both his great love Maud and his wife over the full span of his life. Shakespear clearly meant something – as a friend, as a writer, and as a critic – to Yeats that no one else ever did.

Anne Margaret Daniel
May 2016

NOTES

i   W. B. Yeats, *Memoirs*, transcribed and edited by Denis Dono-
         ghue (London: Macmillan, 1972).

ii   John Harwood, *Olivia Shakespear and W. B. Yeats: After Long
         Silence* (Basingstoke: Macmillan, 1989).

iii   Only a few of Shakespear's letters to Yeats have come to light;
         and she evidently returned his to her when he asked for them,
         as they are with Yeats's family papers.

iv   Roy Foster, *W. B. Yeats: A Life, I: The Apprentice Mage* (Oxford:
         Oxford University Press, 1997) 153.

v   Harwood, *Olivia Shakespear and W. B. Yeats*, 5; 9-10. The prin-
         cipal biographical details of Shakespear's life, unless otherwise
         noted, perforce come from Harwood's careful book about her.

vi   Yeats, *Memoirs*, 87-88.

vii   Richard Ellmann, *Yeats: The Man and The Masks* (1948; New
         York: Norton, 1978) 144; 143.

viii   Olivia Shakespear, *Love on a Mortal Lease* (London: Osgood &
         McIlvaine, 1894) 28-29.

ix   Arthur Waugh to Edmund Gosse, 17 April 1894, in Ann Thwaite,
         Edmund Gosse: A Literary Landscape, 1849-1928 (Chicago: Chicago
         University Press, 1984) 355.

x   Yeats, *Memoirs*, 72.

xi   Foster, *W. B. Yeats*, I, 167.

xii   *The Collected Letters of W. B. Yeats, II, 1896-1900*, edited by
         Warwick Gould, John Kelly and Deirdre Toomey (Oxford:
         Oxford University Press, 1997) 232; 238.

xiii   George Moore, *Evelyn Innes* (1898; New York: Appleton, 1906)
         162-164.

xiv   Letter, Lionel Johnson and Olivia Shakespear to WBY, 8 May
         1894; quoted in Harwood, *Olivia Shakespear and W. B. Yeats*, 37.

xv   Yeats, *Memoirs*, 74.

xvi   Ellmann, *Yeats: Man and Masks*, 168.

xvii   *See ibid.*, 104.

xviii   *The Collected Letters of W. B. Yeats, I, 1865-1895*, edited by John
         Kelly, associate editor Eric Domville (Oxford: Clarendon, 1986)
         136-137.

xix   Yeats, *Memoirs*, 40.

xx   Yeats, *Collected Letters I*, 396-397.

xxi   *ibid.*, 397.

xxii   Foster, *W. B. Yeats*, I, 153.

xxiii   *ibid.*, 155.

xxiv   Yeats, *Memoirs*, 85-86.

xxv   Yeats, *Memoirs*, 86-87.

xxvi   Anna MacBride White and A. Norman Jeffares, eds., *The Gonne-Yeats Letters 1893-1938* (New York: Norton, 1992) 53.

xxvii   *Gonne-Yeats Letters*, 55.

xxviii   Yeats, *Memoirs*, 87.

xxix   Yeats, *Memoirs*, 88.

xxx   Foster, *W. B. Yeats*, I, 157.

xxxi   *ibid.*, 91.

xxxii   *The Savoy*, January 1896, 83.

xxxiii   *The Savoy*, January 1896, 138.

xxxiv   Harwood, *Olivia Shakespear and W. B. Yeats*, 55.

xxxv   Yeats, *Memoirs*, 89.

xxxvi   John Masefield in E.H. Mikhail, ed., *W. B. Yeats: Interviews and Recollections*, 2 vols. (London: Macmillan, 1977) I, 47; quoted in part in Harwood, *Olivia Shakespear and W. B. Yeats*, 54.

xxxvii   Yeats, *Collected Letters II*, 7 n.3, quoting a letter from Symons to Yeats, Sept 26, 1899, reminding Yeats that he still hadn't paid Symons for these items.

xxxviii   James Pethica, ed., *Lady Gregory's Diaries 1892-1902* (Gerrards Cross: Colin Smythe, 1996) 160.

xxxix   Yeats, *Memoirs*, 88.

xl   Yeats, *Collected Letters II*, 34 n.1.

xli   *Gonne-Yeats Letters*, 58.

xlii   *Gonne-Yeats Letters*, 60.

xliii   *Gonne-Yeats Letters*, 62.

xliv   Yeats, *Memoirs*, 104.

xlv   Olivia Shakespear, *The False Laurel* (London: Osgood, 1896) 246.

xlvi   Yeats, *Collected Letters*, *II*, 108.

xlvii   Arthur Symons, *Selected Letters 1880-1935*, edited by Karl Beckson and John M. Munro (London: Macmillan, 1989) 131.

xlviii   John Butler Yeats, *Letters to his Son W. B. Yeats and Others, 1869-1922*, edited by Joseph Hone (London: Faber, 1944) 151-152; *see also* Joseph Hone, *W. B. Yeats 1865-1939* (New York: St. Martin's, 1962) 131.

xlix   Yeats, *Collected Letters*, *II*, 83n.

l   Ellmann, *Yeats: Man and Masks*, 150.

li   Yeats, *Memoirs*, 89.

lii   *ibid.* 89.

liii   Ellmann, *Yeats: Man and Masks*, 85.

liv   *ibid.*, preface xxiv.

lv   Foster, *W. B. Yeats*, I, 437.

lvi   George Mills Harper, *Yeats's Golden Dawn: The Influence of the Hermetic Order of the Golden Dawn on the Life and Art of W. B. Yeats* (Basingstoke: Macmillan, 1974) 27; 105.

lvii   Deirdre Toomey, "'Worst Part of Life': Yeats's Horoscopes for Olivia Shakespear," *Yeats Annual* No. 6, edited by Warwick Gould (London: Macmillan 1988) 223-224; see also Harwood, *Olivia Shakespear and W. B. Yeats*, 91-93.

lviii   Harwood, *Olivia Shakespear and W. B. Yeats*, 90.

lix   Warwick Gould, "Books by Yeats in Olivia Shakespear's Library," *Yeats Annual* No. 9, edited by Deirdre Toomey (Basingstoke: Macmillan, 1992) 301.

lx   Conversation with collector/owner, and viewing of scanned book and inscription, New York, July 2008.

lxi   Yeats, *Collected Letters*, II, 529-530.

lxii   Harwood, *Olivia Shakespear and W. B. Yeats*, 109.

lxiii   Harwood, *Olivia Shakespear and W. B. Yeats*, 111.

lxiv   Humphrey Carpenter, *A Serious Character: The Life of Ezra Pound* (New York: Delta, 1988) 105.

lxv   *The Collected Letters of W. B. Yeats*, III, *1901-1904*, edited by John Kelly and Ronald Schuchard (Oxford: Clarendon, 1994) 628; 633.

lxvi   Foster, *W. B. Yeats*, I, 533-7 (536 [appendix]).

lxvii   See Foster, *W. B. Yeats*, I, 437.

lxviii   Carpenter, *Pound*, 103.

lxix   Carpenter, *Pound*, 221.

lxx   Foster, *W. B. Yeats*, I, 504.

lxxi   Carpenter, *Pound*, 236.

lxxii   W. B. Yeats to Mabel Beardsley, c. Jan. 7, 1915, Beardsley Collection, Princeton University Libraries; quoted in part in Roy Foster, *W. B. Yeats: A Life, II: The Arch-Poet* (Oxford: Oxford University Press, 2003) 6.

lxxiii   Omar Pound, conversations in the Annex Restaurant, Nassau Street, Princeton, New Jersey, 1992-1994.

lxxiv   W. B. Yeats, Diary, December 1914, ms (National Library of Ireland, Michael B. Yeats Papers), quoted in Harwood, *Olivia Shakespear and W. B. Yeats*, 101.

lxxv   W. B. Yeats, *The Letters of W. B. Yeats*, edited by Allan Wade (London: Rupert Hart-Davis, 1954) 715; 748; 698.

lxxvi   John Harwood, ed., "Olivia Shakespear: Letters to W. B. Yeats," *Yeats Annual* No. 6, ed. Warwick Gould (Basingstoke: Macmillan, 1988) 59-107; 71.

lxxvii Yeats, *Letters* (Wade), 818; 854; 603-4; 628; 681.

lxxviii *ibid.*, 916.

lxxix W. B. Yeats, *Letters to Katharine Tynan*, edited by Roger McHugh (Dublin: Clonmore and Reynolds, 1953) 26.

lxxx W. B. Yeats, *The Autobiography of W. B. Yeats* [1938] (New York: Collier Macmillan 1965) 289.

ABOUT THE EDITOR

Anne Margaret Daniel was born and raised in Virginia. She teaches literature at the New School University in New York City. Her articles, essays, notes, and reviews, covering topics from Oscar Wilde's trials to Bob Dylan and contemporary music, have appeared for the past twenty years in books, critical editions, magazines, and journals from *The New York Times* to Hot Press to *The Times Literary Supplement*. She is currently working on a book about F. Scott Fitzgerald. Anne Margaret lives in Manhattan and in upstate New York with her husband.

INTRODUCTION*

Beauty's Hour and its place in *The Savoy*, August/September 1896

The August issue of *The Savoy* was left rather untended, one feels, by its editor and his close collaborator. Arthur Symons and W. B. Yeats had headed to Ireland together, where they spent most of their time in the west. They enjoyed the hospitality of Yeats's relatives in Sligo, and of Edward Martyn at Tillyra Castle, County Galway; and were hosted for lunch by Augusta, Lady Gregory at nearby Coole Park. Back in London, *The Savoy* followed a pattern now visible by its fourth number. An Aubrey Beardsley cover, with far less detail than his earlier drawings for the magazine, features a robed figure celebrating a heap of gathered grapes piled atop a fantastical pedestal. More watercolors by William Blake, not widely published before, accompany Yeats's continuing Blake series, drawn from the three-volume edition of Blake he and Edwin Ellis had spent years preparing for Bernard Quaritch (1893). There are also drawings by Will Horton, Ellis's concluding article of a series on Nietzsche (which does not expand upon his initial point that Nietzsche was a man of genius, but insane), and poems and prose by Ernest Dowson and by Symons.

Most of the stories, from George Morley's "Two Foolish Hearts" to Dowson's "The Dying of Francis Donne," deal with disappointment in love, and/or death. Symons's poem "Stella Maligna" is a morbid mix of decadent sentiment and symbol, much of it borrowed from Yeats. A woman's song to the "little slave" who is her poisoned, drunken lover ("Yet shalt thou live by that delicious death/Thou hast drunken from my breath,/Thou didst with my kisses eat"), it ends with the passionate and rather unexpected release of "The secret light that in the lily glows,/ The miracle of the secret rose."[1]

* As this introduction discusses the novella's plot in detail, first-time readers may wish to read *Beauty's Hour* first and return to the introduction afterwards.

Symons's "Causerie," his name for his Editor's Note, is on
Dowson, the (unnamed) young poet with "the face of a demor-
alized Keats," whose "delicate, mournful, almost colourless,
but very fragrant verses" are steeped in the strong essence of
decadence.[2] The poet's initial grace and delicacy, in his work and
life, has sunk to Dorian-Gray depths that he, purportedly not of
a Dorianic temperament, hates, but cannot escape: "That curious love of the sordid, so common an affectation of the modern
decadent, and with him so expressively genuine, grew upon him,
and dragged him into yet more sorry corners of a life which was
never exactly 'gay' to him. And now, indifferent to most things,
in the shipwrecked quietude of a sort of self-exile, he is living, I
believe, somewhere on a remote foreign sea-coast."[3] By summer
1896, Dowson was living in French and Belgian seaside towns and
drinking heavily; he would be dead in four years.

The only surprising and new thing about the August issue,
carrying on into that of September, is Olivia Shakespear's story.
She had published the novels *Love on a Mortal Lease* in 1894 and *The
Journey of High Honour* in 1895, and had been working on *Beauty's
Hour* during those years. Yeats read it in the summer of 1894, and
offered suggestions about it; he was not happy with the character
of Gerald, finding him ill-defined. Gerald remains undefined,
or at least flatly stereotypical, in the published story, although
Shakespear incorporated Yeats's suggestions and language into
the only description of him, for it is not a man's story at all, but
that of a woman – or, perhaps, two women.

Shakespear's story, never reprinted until today, translates the
evil duality in human nature explored by Robert Louis Steven-
son in his popular story of 1886, *Strange Case of Dr. Jekyll and Mr.
Hyde*, into the dilemma of an unattractive woman who wishes
for beauty. Where Jekyll takes drugs to become Edward Hyde,
Mary Gower transforms herself into Mary Hatherley through
her own will and "ardent desire."[4] The difference of appearance
is critical in both Jekyll/Hyde and Gower/Hatherley; yet while
Hyde is always described as evil in expression (or intimated to be
somehow ugly or shocking because of his evil nature), Hatherley
is universally acclaimed as beautiful. Both Hyde and Hatherley
must ultimately be suppressed for the worlds of their stories to

go on "normally," but Hyde is a murder / suicide while Hatherley is kissed gently goodbye, and reburied in the desire of her creator. She simply decides to let her lovely *alter ego* remain interior.

Mary Gower, the plain secretary to Lady Harman, narrates *Beauty's Hour*. She opens the story of "the strange thing that happened" in a classic, stereotypical female pose, gazing into a mirror at her "own unsatisfactory face." Mary works hard at her job, and her fatigue is only complicated and increased by her love for her employer's son, Gerald Harman. She and Gerald share the sort of dangerously joking dialogue Charlotte Brontë puts into the mouths of Jane Eyre and Rochester; they discuss, in witty repartee, "irrelevant matters" like his latest infatuation, Bella Sturgis. Gerald is not taken with some aspects of Bella – "'She's not intellectual, and she's not really sympathetic, and I don't like her one quarter as much as I do you, Mary,' said he" – but Bella is, as her name implies, beautiful.[5] Mary suffers deeply over her inability to compete with Bella in this decidingly important area; her shifts from past to present tense are striking:

> I repeated Gerald's words as I sat before the glass in my bedroom. "To be sure, the face is enough," he had said.
>
> My own face, pale, with no salient points to make it even impressively ugly, gave me back the speech as I uttered it. I have neither eyelashes, nor distinction; I do not look clever, or even amiable; my figure is not worthy of the name; and my hands and feet are hopeless.
>
> The concentrated bitterness of years swept over me; I loved Gerald Harman, as Bella Sturgis, with her perfect face, was incapable of loving; but my love was rendered grotesque by the accident of birth which had made me an unattractive woman. Given beauty, or even the personal fascination which so often persuades one that it is beauty, I could have held my own against the world, in spite of my poverty, my lack of friends, or of social position. As things were, I saw myself condemned to a sordid monotony; ever at a disadvantage; cheated of my youth, and of nearly all life's sweeter pleasures.[6]

Miss Whateley, Mary's landlady who "had been [her] govern-

ess in better days," listens to Mary's musing over "how different [her] life would be" if she were "a pretty woman – though
only for a few hours out of the twenty-four" – and quite suddenly Mary's wish is fulfilled as she looks again into the mirror.
"[S]omething unforeseen happened: Miss Whateley, standing
behind me, saw it; and I saw it myself as in a dream. My reflected
face grew blurred, and then faded out; and from the mist there
grew a new face, of wonderful beauty; the face of my desire. It
looked at me from the glass, and when I tried to speak, its lips
moved too."[7] Mary's body changes to match her new face:[8]

> My voice was the same; but when I glanced down at my
> body, I saw that it had also undergone transformation. It
> struck me, in the midst of my immense surprise, as being
> curious that I should not be afraid. No explanation of the
> miracle offered itself to me; none seemed necessary: an effort
> of will had conquered the power of my material conditions,
> and I controlled them; my body fitted to my soul at last.
>   "I'm going mad!" cried poor Miss Whateley.
>   "We can't both be mad," said I. "Don't be afraid; tell me
> what I look like."
>   "You are perfectly beautiful," she gasped.
>   I began walking up and down the room: I was much taller,
> and my dress hung clear of my ankles; when I noticed that,
> I began to laugh.

Mary and Miss Whateley mark down the exact hour and date
of the transformation; it is just after sunset. Although Miss Whateley urges her to "wish yourself back," Mary expresses instead
her wish to remain beautiful. They lie to the servant, Jane, telling
her Mary is out and a beautiful stranger is coming to dinner; Jane,
dazzled and tongue-tied, serves them, without remotely recog-
nizing Mary. The women stay up all night, drinking strong tea
and wondering if Mary's transformation will last. It does not. At
"the hour of sunrise," says Mary, "I felt a sensation as of being in
darkness, in thick cloud; from which I emerged with my beauty
fallen from me like a garment fallen from me like a garment . . . I
was conscious only of a physical craving for rest and sleep, which
overpowered me."[9]

Invited to the Harmans' ball as an observer for the spoiled Harman daughters, Mary determines to transform herself again into her "other" for the evening. She has named the beautiful Mary "Mary Hatherley," for "Hatherley had been [her] mother's maiden name."[10] Miss Whateley, however, complicates the situation by insisting they involve a man, and science. They consequently visit one Dr. Trefusis. The good doctor was Mary's father's great friend, her mother's admirer, and her own benefactor. When Mary arrives at his home in the form of Mary Hatherley, he will not believe she is (or is also) Mary Gower. Trefusis's "determination not to recognize me" threatens Mary's "sense of identity" in what she already sees as her true manifestation; Mary is constrained to induce a partial transformation back into plain Mary Gower to convince him.[11]

I held out my right hand – long and beautiful; with delicate fingers, that yet were full of nervous strength.

"That," said I, "is not the hand of Mary Gower." He shrugged his shoulders.

"It is not," said he.

"Look at it," I cried.

Then came an awful moment during which I concentrated my whole will in a passion of energy; the room went black; I was dimly conscious that Dr. Trefusis had fallen on his knees by the table; and I was watching the hand I held under the lamp, with suspended breath; for it had begun to change; some subtle difference passed over it, like a cloud over the face of the sun: its beauty of line and colour faded; the long fingers shrunk, and widened; the blue-veined whiteness darkened into a coarser tint; the fine nails lost their shape, and grew ugly, stunted, and opaque.

The doctor cannot explain Mary's transformation scientifically at all. However, he insists upon seeing her every day – as he is smitten by the apparition – and agrees swiftly to go as her chaperon to the ball, kissing "Mary Hatherley" good night and insisting "I would do anything for a pretty woman."[12] Miss Hatherley is to appear as his niece, a mysterious artist who paints by day and goes out at night.

Like Cinderella, Mary Hatherley is a smashing success at the ball. Gerald is smitten, declaring "Yours is the face I have been looking for all my life," and he ignores Bella.[13] Yet no one listens to what Mary says; they only stare at her, making her extremely uncomfortable with the beauty she has so desired. She is struck by the paradoxes she sees in their behavior: "there was unreality in the air, and a glamour, and an aching pain. Men and women said gracious things to me; yet seemed to watch me with cruel faces; I was only conscious, at the last, of an imperative desire to fly, to hide myself, to escape even from Gerald's presence, and to be alone."[14]

Section II of the story opens the September *Savoy*. The beauty of Miss Hatherley has infatuated not only Gerald, but the whole Harman household. Mary enjoys hearing them talk about her beauty, and decides to go on being Mary Hatherley in the evenings despite Miss Whateley's warnings: "I am at last seeing life as a woman ought to see it. I can't give up the privilege; at least not yet."[15] Mary goes with the Harmans to see *Romeo and Juliet,* and, during the most celebrated tragedy of lovers in English literature, begins to think about the effect Mary Hatherley is having upon Gerald. She possesses two things he has written, one a brief missive to Mary Gower about business of his mother's, and the other an impassioned statement of love to Mary Hatherley. Comparing the two notes, Mary reflects sadly that Gerald, like all men, "can only see inspiration in eyes that are beautiful". Gerald loves "the same woman, with two faces; the woman counts for nothing; the face determines my life ... a man sees only with the outer, never with the inner eye." Weeping at this realization, and at her own lack of surprise about it, Mary announces to her landlady, "There's going to be no transformation tonight, Whatty. I'm tired of masquerading; I am very tired of life. I was born too serious."[16]

When Gerald confesses to Mary Gower that he has fallen in love with a woman who reminds him "in some strange way" of her, she cannot resist. She changes her mind, and decides to resume the character of Mary Hatherley by night. Miss Hatherley remains proud and unresponsive, while Gerald explores London museums and sets about "improving his mind" so as to render himself an acceptable mate to the remarkable, beautiful artist. Mary Gower comes to realize by daytime that she despises her powerful *alter ego*: "I grew to hate the other Mary's beautiful face; her smile; the gracious turn of her head; her shapely hands: I grew to hate all this with a passionate intensity that frightened me ... she was the woman I should have been, and was not." Upon witnessing Bella Sturgis weeping at Gerald's rejection, Mary Gower is conscience-stricken with "[s]hame and an aching remorse" at the pain Mary Hatherley has caused another woman. She extracts from Bella the promise to "be kind" to Gerald, and determines that she will never transform into Mary Hatherley again.[17]

Dr. Trefusis's (Yeatsian) determination that Mary Hatherley is an evil, alchemical conjuration leads him to second this opinion, insisting that "young Harman ought not to be sacrificed to your love of experimentalizing." In a final speech, he asks Mary to come and be his daughter instead – "I promise you I'll age rapidly, and then you'll find you are fulfilling a duty – a sensation dear to the soul of a woman, I know" – and she agrees to this bleak and passionless, but safe, prospect. Having pronounced her own sentence of condemnation on Mary Hatherley, she kisses Gerald goodbye that night and urges him through his protestations to "go back to Bella; for you loved her." Alone in her room, Mary waits for morning, looking at her beautiful self; "and when the dawn came I kissed the wonderful reflected face of Mary Hatherley, and wished her a long good-bye." The face of her dreams is gone; her hour of beauty is over. Mary Gower now wishes, rather like a George Eliot heroine, only to "decline into the lesser ways of life," where not beauty, but peace, may be found.[18]

NOTES

1   *The Savoy*, August 1896, Vol, IV, 64-65.
2   *Savoy IV* 91-2.
3   *Savoy IV* 93.
4   *Savoy IV* 18.
5   *Savoy IV* 11.

6   *Savoy* IV 12.

7   *Savoy* IV 12.

8   *Savoy* IV13-14.

9   *Savoy* IV 14.

10 *Savoy* IV 18.

11 *Savoy* IV 19.

12 *Savoy* IV 21.

13 *Savoy* IV 23.

14 *Savoy* IV 24.

15 *Savoy* V 12.

16 *Savoy* V 16.

17 *Savoy* V 20; 22.

18 *Savoy* V 23; 24; 27.

ACKNOWLEDGEMENTS

I first read Olivia Shakespear as a graduate student at Princeton, working with Elaine Showalter. Deirdre Toomey passionately explained to me one sunny afternoon in Sligo, Ireland, why Shakespear's novels should be back in print. My mother, Margaret Daniel, taught me to read. This book is for Elaine, Deirdre, and Margaret. James Pethica's advice and assistance were, and are, vital. I thank Henry Bergman and Piper Graham for their help in preparing the text.

NOTE ON THE TEXT

The text of this edition follows the first (and only) edition of *Beauty's Hour*, as serialized in *The Savoy* in August and September 1896. In some instances the highly idiosyncratic punctuation of the original has been lightly edited for the sake of clarity and readability.

BEAUTY'S HOUR

A PHANTASY

CHAPTER I

I remember very well the first time the strange thing happened to me: on a winter's day in January. I reached home tired, and sat down in front of the looking-glass to take off my hat; and remained looking, as I so often do, at my own unsatisfactory face.[1]

Gerald Harman had come up to his mother's study that afternoon, while I was at work after lunch; ostensibly on business; really, because there was a frost which had driven him from Leicestershire to London, leaving him with nothing to do; and we had begun talking of irrelevant matters.

"A woman must be good," he said reflectively.

"Only a plain woman," said I. "Who has been behaving ill now?"

"I was generalizing; or, to be frank, I was thinking of Bella Sturgis."

"So am I. You surely don't expect her to possess all the virtues, *and* that face?"

"To be sure, the face is enough," answered he; and sat staring full at me, but thinking, as I knew, of Bella Sturgis.

"Does she amuse you?" I asked.

"Amuse me?" said Gerald. "I'm sure I can't say. One doesn't think about being amused when one is with her."

"She just exists, and that's enough," I suggested.

Possibly my voice was ironical; for Gerald looked at me then, with a sort of jerk.

"She's not intellectual, and she's not really sympathetic, and

I don't *like* her one quarter as much as I do you, Mary," said he.[2]

Now it is an understood thing that he is not to call me Mary, and so I reminded him; but he only answered that we had been over the ground before, and that it was time I owned myself defeated. I was beginning to remark that nothing short of death would induce me to do so, when Lady Harman came in, and Gerald was somewhat abruptly dismissed.

"I wish that idle, mischievous boy would marry Bella, and settle down," said she.

"Yes," said I, and went on writing.

"Why, Mary, how ill you look!" she cried then. "Is anything the matter?"

I hate being told I look ill; it only means that I look ugly: but I answered cheerfully, "Nothing in the world," and she, being easily satisfied, went off to another subject, which lasted till it was time for me to go away. The post of secretary to Lady Harman was not altogether a bed of roses: she has a wide range of interests, and a soft heart; but her other faculties are not quite in proportion. I was generally weary, by the time I reached home, with the endeavour to reconcile her promises and her practice in the eyes of the world—that most censorious of worlds, the philanthropic.

I repeated Gerald's words as I sat before the glass in my bedroom. "To be sure, the face is enough," he had said.

My own face, pale, with no salient points to make it even impressively ugly, gave me back the speech as I uttered it. I have neither eyelashes, nor distinction; I do not look clever, or even amiable; my figure is not worthy of the name; and my hands and feet are hopeless.[3]

The concentrated bitterness of years swept over me; I loved Gerald Harman, as Bella Sturgis, with her perfect face, was incapable of loving, but my love was rendered grotesque by the accident of birth which had made me an unattractive woman. Given beauty, or even the personal fascination which so often persuades one that it is beauty, I could have held my own against the world, in spite of my poverty, my lack of friends, or of social position. As things were, I saw myself condemned to a sordid monotony —ever at a disadvantage; cheated of my youth, and of nearly all life's sweeter possibilities. I was considered clever, by the Harmans, it is true; but the world in general, had it noticed me at all, would have refused to believe that such a face as mine could harbour brains. Gerald, I knew, had proclaimed in the family that Mary Gower had wits, and looked on me as his own special discovery; for though I had but a plain head on my shoulders, it was an accurate thinking machine; and could occasionally produce a phrase worthy of his laughter.[4]

I have a certain dreary sense of humour which prevents my being, as a rule, quite overwhelmed by this aspect of my life; but on the January afternoon of which I write, I was fairly mastered by it; and when Miss Whateley came up to light the gas, which she generally did herself, she found me with my head on the dressing-table, in an attitude of abject despair. Miss Whateley was my landlady, and had been my governess in better days.[5]

"My dear," said she, "what's the matter?"

"Only my face," said I.

"Glycerine is the best thing," said she, and began pulling the curtains.

She knew perfectly well what I meant.

"Whatty," said I, musingly, "how different my life would be if I were a pretty woman—though only for a few hours out of the twenty-four."

"Oh, yes," she answered. "Yet you might be glad sometimes when the hours were over."

I only shook my head; and fell to looking into my own eyes again, with the yearning, stronger than it had ever been before, rising like a passion into my face.

Then something unforeseen happened: Miss Whateley, standing behind me, saw it; and I saw it myself as in a dream. My reflected face grew blurred, and then faded out; and from the mist there grew a new face, of wonderful beauty; the face of my desire. It looked at me from the glass, and when I tried to speak, its lips moved too. Miss Whateley uttered a sound that was hardly a cry, and caught me by the shoulder.

"Mary—Mary—" she said.

I got up then and faced her; she was white as death, and her eyes were almost vacant with terror.

"What has happened?" said I.

My voice was the same; but when I glanced down at my body, I saw that it also had undergone transformation. It struck me, in the midst of my immense surprise, as being curious that I should not be afraid. No explanation of the miracle offered itself to me; none seemed necessary: an effort of will had conquered the power of my material conditions, and I controlled them; my body fitted to my soul at last.[6]

"I'm going mad!" cried poor Miss Whateley.

"We can't both be mad," said I. "Don't be afraid; tell me what I look like."

"You are perfectly beautiful," she gasped.

I began walking up and down the room. I was much taller, and my dress hung clear of my ankles; when I noticed that, I began to laugh.

"Whatty, I've grown," I cried out.

She sat down. "Do you feel strange?" she asked.

"Just the same; only a little larger for my clothes. What are we going to do? Will it last?"

"I think you had better just sit down again, and wish yourself back."

"Never, never. If beautiful I can be, beautiful I will remain. Let us put down the hour and the date."

I took up my diary, and made a great cross against the day; then I noticed that the sun set at twenty-seven minutes past four; it was now twenty-five minutes to five.

"I wonder what we can do to prove to ourselves that we've not been dreaming, if I go back again?" I questioned.

"Let us first spend the evening as usual," answered Miss Whateley. "I will tell Jane that you are out, and that a young lady is coming to supper with me."

Jane was our one servant. Her powers of observation were limited, and we did not think it would be difficult to deceive her. So the stranger, whose appearance seemed to bereave her of even her usual small allowance of sense, sat that night at Miss Whateley's table; at ten o'clock we slipped up to my bedroom; and when Jane's tread was heard in the room above, we breathed freely.

"She's gone to bed," said I. "Now we can brew tea, and keep ourselves awake. We must not sleep; that is imperative."

We did not sleep; though to poor Miss Whateley, who had no sense of a triumphant new personality to sustain her, the task must have been difficult.[7]

Then, suddenly, at the hour of sunrise, I felt a sensation as of being in darkness, in thick cloud; from which I emerged with my beauty fallen from me like a garment.[8]

We neither of us said anything. I was conscious only of a physical craving for rest and sleep, which overpowered me. I think Miss Whateley was struck dumb in the presence of a wonder she could not understand. We kissed one another silently, and I went to bed and slept for a couple of hours, a dreamless sleep.

CHAPTER II

When I reached Lady Harman's that morning, I found the two girls, Clara and Betty, alone in their mother's study.

Betty, with the face of a Romney, and the manners of an engaging child, is wholly attractive.[9] Clara is handsome too; she rather affects a friendship with me on intellectual grounds, which bores me: her theories are the terror of my life, being always in direct opposition to my own, for which I have to try and account.

But on this particular morning she had nothing more momentous on her mind than a dance, which her mother was giving the next evening.

"You *must* come to it," Betty cried. "It will be such fun talking it over afterwards. Onlookers always see most of the game, you know."

"You are very kind, Betty," I said. They had long ago insisted that I should call them by their Christian names. "Has it ever struck you that onlookers would sometimes like to be in the game, instead of outside it?"

Betty looked a little confused.

"Well, somebody must look on," said she. "And it's lucky when they see how funny things are, as you always do, Mary."

"Is there any particular game going on just now?" I inquired. "Can I be of any use?"

"There's Bella," said both girls.

I was very anxious to know the precise sum of Bella's iniquities. I shoved away my papers with an entire lack of conscience; and sat expectant.

"Of course Bella is very young," Clara began: she being about twenty-one herself. "One mustn't judge her too hardly."

"Has she been doing anything you would not have done yourself?" I asked.

Betty looked at me, and raised her eyebrows. Clara was apt to pose as an example to her younger sister.

"Well," said Clara, "*if* I were engaged to some one as nice as

Gerald, and handsome, and well off, and all the rest of it, I don't think I'd encourage a little wretch like Mr. Trench."

Clara's social ethics are of a wonderful simplicity.

"Because you'd think it wrong?" I suggested.

"Well—so silly," said Clara.

"I think Bella has a perfect right to do as she likes," broke in Betty. "She's *not* engaged to Gerald; he hasn't proposed to her; and he ought to, for she's awfully fond of him."

"I agree with you both," said I. "Miss Sturgis is silly, but not altogether to be blamed. Am I to observe her and Mr. Trench together, and report the phases of the flirtation to you?"

Yes: that was what they wanted.

"Do you seriously think I'm coming to your dance?" I went on. "Why, I haven't got a dress, or a face fit to show in a ball-room; and I've not been to a ball for years."

They fought this statement inch by inch: they would lend me a dress; my face didn't matter; and after all, I was only twenty-eight, not really old. I ended the discussion by promising to go, for an idea had flashed into my mind that made me dizzy.[10]

Supposing the other, the beautiful Mary, renewed her existence again that evening, might she not enjoy a strange, a brief triumph? Would there not be a perfect, though a secret pleasure in seeing the look in Gerald Harman's eyes, in surprising the altered tones of his voice? For beauty drew him like a magnet.

I fell into such a deep silence over this thought, that Clara and Betty grew weary, and went away; and I did not see them again till luncheon-time.

There were three visitors: the man who was in love with Betty, and the man with whom Betty was in love; the juxtaposition of the two always delighted me. I don't believe they hated one another; but each believing himself to be the favoured lover, had a fine scorn for the other's folly. The third guest was Bella Sturgis.

Gerald sat at the end of the table, opposite his mother. As I have said, the frost kept him from hunting, and he was disconsolate. With him, as with many finely bred, finely tempered Englishmen, sport was a passion; more, a religion. He put into his hunting, his shooting, his cricket, all the ardour, all the sincerity that are necessary to achievement. I respected this in him, even while it moved me to a kind of pity; for I felt instinctively that though he might have skill and courage to overcome physical difficulties or danger, he was totally unfitted to cope with the more subtile side of life; and would be helpless in the face of an emotional difficulty. On this day of which I write, he was evidently suffering from some jar to the even tenour of his life; of which the continued frost was a merely superficial aggravation.[11]

By his side sat Bella Sturgis. I looked at her with a more critical eye than usual: she had a great air of languid distinction; everything about her was perfect, from the pose of her head to the intonation of her voice. She very rarely looked at me, and I don't think she had ever clearly realized who I was: I felt sure Gerald had not imparted his discoveries to her with regard to my wits. I never spoke at luncheon when she was there.

But to-day, the memory of that face in the glass the night before, made me reckless and audacious.

"I've been constituted the girl's special reporter to-morrow night," said I to Gerald. "I am to observe the faces, and the flirtations."

"Then you may constitute yourself my special reporter too," said he, gloomily.

"It will be the next best thing to dancing," I went on.

"Why don't you dance?" Miss Sturgis asked, lifting her eyes, and looking at me for an instant.

I confess I was a little surprised at the cleverness of her thrust.

"Because nobody asks me," I said, with a smile.

My candour had no effect on her: she turned to Gerald with an air that dismissed the whole subject. I noticed that he would hardly answer her; and I supposed that the breach between them had widened. So she addressed herself to the man with whom Betty was in love, thereby throwing the table into a state of suppressed agitation, with the exception of Lady Harman, who professed to notice none of the details of domestic life: she left such things to the girls, or the servants; and devoted herself to the care of people in Billingsgate, or in the Tropics, who had need of her, she said.[12] But she was really kind; and always had a joint for lunch, "because it was Mary's dinner;" and though I often yearned for the other more interesting dishes, I never dared to suggest any deviation from beef and mutton: to-day it was mutton.[13]

"Won't you have some more?" said Lady Harman. "I can't help thinking how much we waste. Some of my poor families would be so glad of this, and here's only Mary touches it."

"Oh, mother," said Betty, "your poor people are always starving; and a leg more or less wouldn't make much difference."

"What's an arm or a leg, compared with a face?" said the young man who was in love with Betty, with his eyes fixed on her. His remark had no direct bearing on the subject, which he had but half followed; and it sent her into a fit of suppressed laughter, with which Clara remonstrated in an undertone.

"I don't care," said the rebellious Betty. "It's Gerald's house, and as long as he doesn't mind my giggling, I shall giggle."

"I mind nothing," said the master of the house. His mood was obviously overcast. I saw Bella throw a look at him out of her deep eyes; the eyes of a woman who has always lived under emotional conditions. I began to realize dimly what such conditions might be like.

He got up, and pushed his chair from the table.

"Will you excuse me," said he. "I have an engagement."

"Do go," said Lady Harman, "you are always late, Gerald. I'm sure you ought to go at once."

Bella held out her hand to him.

"It's *au revoir*, not good-bye," said he, and did not take it.

That evening my transformation took place again; under the same conditions of ardent desire on my part.

"To-morrow," said I to Miss Whateley, "I shall go to the Harmans' ball in the character of Mary Hatherley." Hatherley had been my mother's maiden name.[14]

"But you have no dress," said Miss Whateley. "And how can you account for yourself?"

"I must do it," I cried. "You must think of some plan."

"Let us go," said she, "to Dr. Trefusis."

CHAPTER III

Dr. Trefusis was the only man who had ever loved me. He was my father's great friend; but I feel sure he must once have been in love with my mother; at least, I can only account for his great affection for myself, on some such sentimental hypothesis. When my father died, four years ago, and I was involved in money difficulties, it was Dr. Trefusis who took me in, and eventually got me my secretaryship with Lady Harman. He wanted me to share his home; but this I refused to do; believing his affection for me could not stand the test of losing his liberty, and his solitude.

When we reached his house, he was out; and we waited some time in the library.

"He won't believe us," Miss Whateley kept saying; and this seemed so likely, that I was shivering with nervousness when he at last came in.

"You won't believe it," said Miss Whateley, "but this is Mary Gower."

He looked very blank; but recovering his presence of mind, turned to me and said,

"A cousin, I presume, of my old friend, Mary Gower?"

"Oh, Dr. Trefusis," cried I, "we have come to you with the most extraordinary story: don't you know my voice? I *am* Mary; but I have got into another body."

"The voice is Mary's," said he, in the tone of one balancing evidence.

Then Miss Whateley began telling him what had happened: while I sat in silence, watching the mixture of wonder and scepticism on his face. I noticed also another look, when his eyes met mine, a look that was almost devout—he had always been a worshipper of beauty.

When the story was done, he began asking questions. My answers seemed unsatisfactory: we sat at last without speaking, while he looked at me, and drummed on the table.

"You are very plausible people," he said, at length, "but you can't expect me to believe all this; though I'm at a loss to imagine why you should take the trouble to play such a practical joke on a poor old fellow like myself. Still, I'll not be ungracious, and grumble; for it has given me a great deal of pleasure to see anything so charming in this dull place."

He got up, as though he wished to end the interview.

I was in despair: his determination not to recognize me struck like a blow at my sense of identity. Then the thought came: could I, by a supreme effort of will, induce a transformation under his very eyes?

I held out my right hand—long and beautiful; with delicate fingers, that yet were full of nervous strength.

"That," said I, "is not the hand of Mary Gower." He shrugged his shoulders.

"It is not," said he.

"Look at it," I cried.

Then came an awful moment during which I concentrated my whole will in a passion of energy. The room went black; I was dimly conscious that Dr. Trefusis had fallen on his knees by the table, and was watching the hand I held under the lamp with suspended breath: for it had begun to change; some subtle difference passed over it, like a cloud over the face of the sun: its beauty of line and colour faded; the long fingers shrunk, and widened; the blue-veined whiteness darkened into a coarser tint; the fine nails lost their shape, and grew ugly, stunted, and opaque.

Dr. Trefusis spoke no word: I felt his fingers were ice-cold as he turned up my sleeve, and noted how the coarsened wrist grew into the perfect arm; he held my hand, and swung it to and fro; then he left the room abruptly, saying "don't move."

I sat still at the table: Miss Whateley came and stood by me.

"Mary," she said, "it must be wrong; it is playing with some terrible power you don't understand."

"Probably we've all got it," I answered dreamily. "It is perhaps a spark of the creative force—but Dr. Trefusis and all his science won't be able to explain it."[15]

Then the doctor came back, with instruments, and microscopes, and I know not what, and began to examine the miracle. At last he looked up at me.

"I can make nothing of it," said he. "But it is the hand of Mary Gower. That is beyond dispute. Now let it go back."

He held it in his own: this time the change was quicker; and he dropped it with a shudder.

"Now do you believe me?" I asked.

He answered, "yes;" and sat lost in thought.

"You had better go home now," he said presently. "I must think over all this; there must be some hypothesis—miracles don't happen—you must let me see you every day."

I never have understood, and never shall understand, the scientific theories which he had first built up, in order to account for what had happened to me. I was grateful for the curiosity and interest that my case roused in him, because they led him to help me in practical ways; but any attempt at a scientific explanation of the mystery struck me as being irrelevant, and not particularly interesting. This attitude on my part at once amused and irritated him; he gave up trying to make me understand the meaning of his investigations; and of the experiments which he made me try; for it was not till later that he came to look upon the matter as beyond any scientific solution; and only to be accounted for on grounds which he would at first have rejected with scorn.

I pass these things over; because I could not write of them intelligibly, and I might be doing Dr. Trefusis some injustice by an imperfect exposition.

On this occasion, I burst in suddenly, and scattered his reflections by declaring that I must go to the Harmans' ball the next night, in my new character.

The idea seemed to divert him.

"Ha!" said he. "Mary Gower wants to taste the sweets of success, does she! Upon my soul, it would be worth seeing you, my dear. But it would be difficult to account for the sudden rising of such a star."

"Not if you took me, and chaperoned, and uncled me," I said.

He took a turn or two in the room.

"Why not?" he said then, with a laugh.

"Oh, Dr. Trefusis, would you really!" I cried out, and seized him by both hands.

He held them and looked at me oddly; he is a man of nearly

sixty, and my old friend; so I could not be angry when he bent down and kissed me.

"I would do anything for a pretty woman," said he.

I felt a sudden pang: this was the first tribute offered to my beauty, and it hurt. Was Mary Gower beginning already to be jealous of Mary Hatherley?

We settled the matter, with jests and laughter. Dr. Trefusis has the spirit of a child, and the capacity for making abrupt transitions from the serious to the absurd; and he now entered into the plot as though it were a game, as though nothing had happened to unnerve and startle him but a short time before. I was to be his niece, a niece from the country; if further inquiries were made, and my non-appearance during the day had to be accounted for, I was to be a devoted art student; an eccentric; who gave her days to painting, and her evenings to pleasure. Miss Whateley's faint objections were soon silenced: we parted with a promise to meet the next morning, when the Harman household would be upset and I should not be wanted, to choose a ball dress.

"Not that that face of yours needs any artificial setting," were his last words.

"I only hope you won't repent all this," were Miss Whateley's, as we went up to bed.

CHAPTER IV

My father had taken me, as a young girl, to balls. I had sat out unnoticed, but observant; and it had seemed to me that, under apparently artificial conditions, women grouped themselves into three distinct types, which were almost primitive in their lack of complexity: the beauty; the woman whose claims to beauty are not universally acknowledged; and the plain woman.

The beauty always pleased me the most: she was unconscious; using her divine right of sovereignty with a carelessness only possible to one born in the purple; experience had bred in her a certainty of pleasing that made her indifferent to the effect she produced, which indifference made her the more effective. That she had her secret moments of scorn, I never doubted; a scorn of that lust of the eye which held her beauty too dear; and I wondered whether any such woman had ever felt tempted in some moment of outraged emotion to curse the loveliness that men loved, careless of the heart, or head.

The woman with disputable claims annoyed me: she seemed to me like a queen dependent on the humour of the mob, from whose brows the uneasy crown might be torn, and trampled under foot; and then replaced at a caprice. She was uncertain of herself; too much affected by the opinions of others to be easy or unconscious. I was sorry for her too; I felt sure that she often married the man who thought her beautiful, out of gratitude; for she was always unduly grateful, her attitude towards the world being one of mingled depreciation and assertion.

As for the plain woman, had I not stood hand in hand with her outside the gates of Paradise all my life, the angel with the two-edged sword looking on us, with eyes that held both pity and satire! Oh, kind angel—stand aside, and let us look through the bars, and see gracious figures going to and fro; and listen to strange music, and to the sound of voices moved by a keen, sweet passion. We look; we fall back; and know the angel by his several names: Fate; Injustice; Mercy.

*

I had always recognized the subtile emotional intoxicant that is distilled from the atmosphere of a ball-room. It seemed to come in great waves about me, as I walked up the Harmans' ball-room, followed by Dr. Trefusis.

He had written for permission to bring his niece, and they were prepared to see me. No, I am wrong; they were not prepared. Lady Harman was visibly taken aback; and Clara and Betty had something deferential in their manner, which showed a desire to be unusually pleasing. Then Gerald came forward. His eyes met mine, with the look of one who sees something he has long sought, and despaired of finding.

"Can you spare me a dance—" he asked, pausing at the name.

"My name is Hatherley," said I.

My voice struck him; he glanced at me with a puzzled expression, and hesitated—for a moment.

"I must have more than one," he said.

That was so like Gerald, I nearly laughed.

"The page is blank, you see," I answered.

He took advantage of my remark, and wrote his name several times in my programme. I have the programme still.

Dancing had begun again: a crowd had emerged from the stairs and the anterooms. A number of men were introduced to me, some of whom I had already seen at the house. The first with whom I danced was a Colonel Weston; I knew him, on Betty's authority, to be a beautiful dancer, but he was a head shorter than I, and I smiled involuntarily when he said, "Shall we dance?"

He caught my smile.

"Why are you so divinely tall, O daughter of the gods?" said he. "And from what Olympian height have you descended this evening? Why have I never met you before?"

"I will answer no questions," said I, "till we have danced. My feet ache to begin."

"Then they don't dance on Olympus?"

"The gods must come among the mortals to make merry," I said.

"For which thing let us be thankful," he answered. Then we moved away. I had been hitherto a bad dancer, but to-night I felt a spirit in my feet, and realized, for the first time, the mysterious joy of perfect motion. As we paused near the door, I saw Bella Sturgis coming slowly up the stairs. She did not take her eyes off me. I saw her question the man on whose arm she was leaning, but he looked at me without answering. It was a revelation, that look in their eyes; I saw it repeated, in other faces, over and over again, as I walked slowly across the ball-room after the dance was over.

The next was with Gerald. My pulses beat thickly, and I was hardly conscious of the outside world, till we stopped dancing, and he led me into a little room, which I did not at the moment recognize as Lady Harman's study.

"And so I have met you at last," he said; and I asked him what he meant.

"Yours is the face I have been looking for all my life," he answered.

There was a strange simplicity in his voice, and words; as though he spoke on an impulse that overruled all conventions, all fear of offence.

"But what of the woman behind the face?" I questioned.

"Can I ever hope to know her?"

"If you know her, you will be disappointed: she is like any other woman."

He shook his head.

"I don't believe it. Tell me what she is really like."

I looked round vaguely, my thoughts intent on what I should say to him: then I suddenly noticed the pictures on the walls, and remembered that this was the room in which Mary Gower sat every day.

"She is not without heart, and she has a head that can think," said I.

"That is not like every other woman."

"Would you credit her with either, if she had another face?" I asked him.

Something in my voice struck him, for the second time. He looked at me with a quickened attention.

"The face is an indication of the soul, surely," he answered.

"That is a lie," said I. "A lie invented to cover the injustice done alike to the beautiful woman, and the woman who is not beautiful."

"Injustice?" he echoed.

"The thing is so simple," said I, with a bitterness I could not hide. "You place beauty on a pedestal; her face is an index to her soul, you say. What happens if you find she does not possess the soul, which she never claimed to have, but which you insisted on crediting her with? You dethrone her with ignominy. The case of the other woman is as hard: she has a face that does not attract you, so you deny her the soul that you forced on the other one. She goes through life, branded; not by individuals, I allow, but by public opinion. The *vox populi* is the voice of nature, 'tis true; but nature is very hard, very ruthless."

I stopped. Gerald sat looking at me, with a rapt gaze, but I saw he had not listened to a word I said. The Hungarian band had begun playing again in the ball-room. As I listened, and watched the phantastic whirl of the dancers through the open door, they seemed to me to symbolize the burden of all the ages: desire and satiety; illusion and reality, dancing hand in hand, to a music wild and tender as love, sad and stern as life—partners that look ever in one another's eyes, and dance on, in despite of what they see.

"Let us go and dance too," said Gerald.

I have no very clear recollection of the rest of that evening —there was unreality in the air, and a glamour, and an aching pain. Men and women said gracious things to me, yet seemed to watch me with cruel faces. I was only conscious, at the last, of an imperative desire to fly, to hide myself, to escape even from Gerald's presence; and to be alone.

CHAPTER V

There was confusion in the Harmans' house the next day. I did no work, but sat idly with the girls in their sitting-room, while they talked over the ball. They were full of the new beauty, Miss Hatherley.

"And such an odd thing, Mary. Gerald says she reminds him of you."

"Quite impossible," said I, "but I thank him."

"Something in her voice and way of talking," Betty went on. "You *have* a nice voice, you know. Gerald says she is very original, and goodness knows he had opportunity enough of finding it out; he danced with no one else."

I nearly contradicted that statement, but saved myself in time.

"I'm so sorry I couldn't go," I said instead. "Did Miss Sturgis enjoy herself?"

"And are you really better?" said Betty. "You didn't seem ill in the afternoon. As for Bella——"

"Oh, Bella!" interrupted Clara. "Bella had best look to her laurels. No one noticed her while Miss Hatherley was in the room."

I went on with my questions.

"Do you suppose Miss Hatherley enjoyed her success?"

They laughed.

"Why, yes, if she's like other girls."

"Perhaps she isn't. Do all girls enjoy being admired at the expense of some one else?"

Clara looked out of the window, with an assumption of unconsciousness. Betty, who is more candid, answered at once, "One can't help liking it."

I laughed outright.

"Does Miss Hatherley seem nice?" I asked next.

"Charming," said Clara. "We have taken quite a fancy to her. Mother is writing to-day to ask her to dine and go to the theatre with us to-morrow. That was Gerald's idea."

I received this piece of news in silence.

"Everyone wants to know her," Clara went on. "Dr. Trefusis was overwhelmed with questions and inquiries as to whether people might call, and so on. She paints all day through; works quite hard, as though she had to do it. Odd, isn't it?"

"Why odd?" said I. "I suppose she likes it. But a passion for art is unnecessary in a pretty woman, no doubt." And Betty broke in with, "Oh, there you go again, Mary! Always finding fault with pretty women."

"Not with them, my dear, but with the world," I said, laughing. "You can't say I find fault with you, Betty."

"Oh, I'm not pretty," said she, "by Miss Hatherley."

I was touched by her speech.

"You're a generous creature," I said. "I have always supposed it a mistake to think that one pretty girl is jealous of another."

Betty put her head on one side, and, with an odd mixture of wisdom and drollery, answered, "Well, we like beauty—and we don't. We like it because it's interesting, and exciting, and successful; and a pretty girl gives one's house a certain reputation. We don't approve when she annexes people who belong to us, naturally; all the same, we can't help feeling she must do as she pleases—she's privileged."

"I had no idea you were so profound," said Clara, a little sharply; and I wondered whether it is possible that women are more tenacious of an intellectual than of a physical superiority.

Betty only laughed.

"I'm off," said she. "I promised to meet the Sturgises in the park; but Gerald won't come, and I'm half afraid to face Bella alone. Good-bye, Mary. We'll ask you to meet Miss Hatherley when we know her better."

When I got home I found that Dr. Trefusis had sent on Lady Harman's letter. I sat over it for some time, thinking; then I wrote and said I would go. Miss Whateley looked at me wistfully when I told her.

"I'm afraid you will get into some trouble, Mary," she said, "and you can't possibly wear the ball dress."

"I must go," I retorted. "I am at last seeing life as a woman ought to see it. I can't give up the privilege; at least not yet."

"You won't give it up till you have paid the penalty," Miss Whateley answered.

I shrugged my shoulders, as though I did not believe her.

"I must have another dress," I cried.

Miss Whateley would have given me the clothes off her back, she said; but as that would not avail me much, she offered to lend me some money. I accepted the offer with a recklessness born of my strange position; and we went out shopping, after sunset, Mary Hatherley and Miss Whateley.[16]

The people in the shops seemed anxious to please me, even when they found that I could afford to pay but little for what I wanted. They probably looked upon me as a good advertisement, and I enjoyed the novelty of being treated with a deferential consideration.

It was a very cold night; as we passed along the freezing, gas-lit streets we met but few people. We had to cross the square in which Dr. Trefusis lived on our way home. I noticed, before we reached his door, that a man in a fur overcoat was pacing slowly up and down the pavement. Why did he linger in such weather? I wondered vaguely. Then I saw it was Gerald Harman. I put my muff up to my face and passed him by. I knew, too well, that he was waiting on the chance of seeing Mary Hatherley on her way home from a day's work at the studio.

"You do not work very late these foggy days, I suppose?" he asked me, tentatively, the next evening at dinner.

"I make gaslight studies," said I, shortly.

"Is it permitted to anybody to go and see you at work?"

"Oh no," I answered, with a smile. "I paint in earnest."

"I waited an hour in Dorchester Square last night," he went on, very low, "in the hope of seeing you."[17]

"That was misplaced heroism," said I, "in such weather. I should advise you not to do it again."

"I shall do it every evening," he declared; and I only laughed a little, as though the subject were not of the remotest interest, and turned to my neighbour.

Gerald sat by me at the play. I went so seldom to the theatre that I was always arrested by the interest of the piece, and of the actors. I sat in the front of the box by Lady Harman, who, I was certain, suffered under the uneasy sensation that she was taking a leap in the dark in encouraging a young unknown woman, with nothing to recommend her but her looks; though, on the other hand, she was upheld by the authoritative voice of society, which had pronounced a favourable verdict on me.

Behind us were Gerald and Betty. It was such an intimate family party that I had great difficulty in not using the familiar tone of every day. When I had only just saved myself from calling Betty by her Christian name, and pointing out an acquaintance of Gerald's, whom I knew by sight, in the stalls, I was sobered.

Silence fell upon me: I was so acutely aware of Gerald's presence, which seemed like a light at which I could not bear to look, that I tried to distract myself by noting the faces of the other people in the house till the curtain should rise. Here and there I caught glimpses of a pretty head, the graceful turn of a neck, an expression of happiness or of vivacity; but the audience was mostly ugly, dull, and uninteresting. Yet I felt sorry for all these people; for their inarticulate dumb way of going through life, untouched by passion, save in its baser aspects, and only apprehending the ideal through some conventionalized form of religion, or some dim discontent.

The play was "Romeo and Juliet": the Juliet was beautiful, but she could only look the part; and the young man who acted Romeo was no ideal lover; yet the immortal, golden play of youth and passion drew tears, and quickened heartbeats; for each woman in the house was Juliet, tasting some rapture, perhaps lost, perhaps never realized, of first love.[18]

The curtain dropped: I sat in a dream, and Lady Harman's voice seemed to come from very far away.

"It's a pretty play," she said. "But don't you think it's rather a muddle? I never can make out who is who."

"It doesn't matter," answered Betty. "Don't trouble, mother dear. What a lovely thing it would be for private theatricals, parts of it, that is. Gerald, wouldn't Bella make a good Juliet?"

Her remark might, or might not have been malicious, but Gerald started. "Bella!" he ejaculated, and looked at me. His look said plainly what his lips had not yet dared; no man had ever yet looked at me with entreaty, passion, humility, in his eyes. I looked back at him, the soul of Mary Gower speaking through the eyes of Mary Hatherley. He flushed, and went pale again, and I regretted what I had done. For the rest of the evening I devoted myself to Lady Harman: Gerald seemed lost in thought, and only roused himself when the carriage stopped at Dr. Trefusis' door.

"I shall never see you alone," said he, as we stood on the doorstep. "I cannot talk to you—I must write to you," he ended, with a sort of despairing impatience.

"Do not write," said I: and then the door was opened by the doctor in person. Gerald seemed hardly able to speak to him; when a few words had passed he went back abruptly to the carriage.

"Mary," said Dr. Trefusis, "you are a great trouble to me. Now I've got to take you home, and interrupt my studies in Rosenkrantz and the Pope Honorius, most absorbing old impostors —no, I won't say that; for I'm beginning to think there may be some method in their madness.[19] You have led me into devious paths, Mary Hatherley. By the way, who's that good-looking young fellow?"

"That's Gerald Harman," said I.

The doctor looked at me with a sort of inquisitive sympathy; and shrugged his shoulders. When he left me at my own house, "You are playing with fire, my dear," he said, "and I'm an old fool to help you."

"You are helping me to buy the experience that teaches," I said, "and it teaches bitter lessons enough: don't fear for me."

CHAPTER VI

I had never received a love-letter; and the only scrap of Gerald Harman's writing that I possessed was a little note, which said:

"Dear Miss Gower, my mother asks me to write and tell you that she will be back to-morrow, and expects you on Thursday as usual. Yours very truly,

"GERALD HARMAN."

I sat comparing this letter with the letter he had written to Mary Hatherley, and I do not think I have ever known a more miserable moment.

"I ought to begin by asking you to forgive me," the letter ran. I am afraid of your thinking me too bold in writing; yet you must know that love comes sometimes in a sort of flash that makes one see life quite differently in a moment. That is what happened to me the first time I ever saw you. Since then I have thought of nothing else. If you would be kind, if you would care what becomes of me, I might be able to make a better thing of life. I have been very idle and useless always, and now I feel ashamed of it. I dare not ask if you could ever care for me—not yet. You know how I love you, and am ever yours

"GERALD HARMAN."

I was sitting in my bedroom, at the little dressing-table which did duty for a writing-table too. I looked again into my own eyes in the glass, as I had done on that memorable evening that seemed such a very long while ago. We knew one another's bitterness, my reflection and I, and laughed aloud.

"Man's love," said I to the face in the glass, "man's humility, man's cry of 'trample on me, and re-mould me,' what does it all amount to? Here am I; the same woman, with two faces. The woman counts for nothing; the face determines my life. A man can only see inspiration in eyes that are beautiful; words can only influence him when the lips that say them have curves and a smile that delight. I, Mary Gower, could love him, could help him, as far as my soul and will go; but he cannot see this: a man sees only with the outer, never with the inner eye."

"Perhaps we are unjust," I went on again presently. "There are, no doubt, men to whom the outside of a woman is not the whole; but they must have learnt discernment, either through some special suffering, or they are perhaps lacking in sensuous instincts, and care but little for women at all, either from the intellectual or the emotional side. Gerald is not one of these; he is like other men; his point of view may be fairly taken as representing a normal one—and he loves Mary Hatherley!"

"Come in," I went on, in answer to a knock at the door. "There's going to be no transformation to-night, Whatty. I'm tired of masquerading; I am very tired of life. I was born too serious. I can't live in the passing hour, and enjoy it; I think of yesterday, and of to-morrow. Why can't I fling all care to the winds and make merry, with the other Mary's beautiful face, and all it brings me!"

Miss Whateley put her hands on my shoulder, and I turned to her, and wept.

I did not answer Gerald's letter; nor did I see him till a few days later, when he strolled into Lady Harman's study in his usual careless way.

"I'm out of sorts, Mary," said he. "Let me sit here, while you talk to me. I like the sound of your voice."

I knew why he liked the sound of my voice, and it hardened me against him.

"Why out of sorts?" said I. "Haven't you eaten, drunk, and been merry? What more does a man want?"

"I've eaten less, drunk considerably more, and not been in the least merry," he answered. "Just now I wish that I might die— to-morrow, or even to-day."

I looked at him with a sudden pity mixed with my anger—that pity which is at once the root and the flower of love.

"You are unhappy, really?" I asked, knowing that Mary Hatherley had not answered his letter.

"I'm miserable!" he cried out.

Then he began walking up and down the room, and I felt, with a quickening of fear and interest, that he was going to speak to me of her. I yielded then to a strange impulse, which was almost like jealousy of myself.

"What has Bella Sturgis been doing?" said I.

He stopped dead.

"Bella . . . she seems to have drifted a thousand miles away. She belongs to the old life, from which I am cut off. There's a gulf opened between me and it; she is on the other side."

"I don't understand, then," said I.

"O Mary," Gerald cried, "I'm very hard hit this time! Haven't you heard of Mary Hatherley?"

"Tell me about her," I said.

There was a great fire in the room, and I sat close to it; but my hands were like ice. Gerald leant against the mantelpiece, and looked down on me. He was full of that intoxicating spirit of youth and enthusiasm, which carries such an irresistible appeal to those whose own youth is clouded, and who cannot rise above a resigned cheerfulness. Even now, when he declared himself to be miserable, there was an ardour in his discouragement which made it almost a desirable emotion.

"Mary Hatherley," he began, "reminds me in some strange way of you: she says things so like what you say, and the very voice is like."

"But she's very lovely," I interposed. "And you've fallen seriously in love at last?"

He did not resent my remark.

"Seriously—at last," he answered, with a smile.

"Why have you never fallen in love with me?" I asked then.

He began to laugh, with genuine amusement.

"You're an amazing person," said he. "I shall, if you're not careful."

"Well, but why not?" I persisted. "It's true that I am only your mother's secretary, but you say I'm like Miss Hatherley in my ideas and way of talking. Is it the face that makes the difference?"

"I know you are following up something infernally abstruse," said he, "that has no relation to the facts of life; that's so like you.

I daresay the face *does* make a difference: it makes a difference in the whole personality."

"I wanted to find out the facts," said I. "And you have given me a fairly direct answer, which can serve as a premise from which I shall draw my conclusions."

"And your conclusions are——?"

"That justice is an ironical goddess, whose eyes are never really bandaged."

"Your vein is too deep for me to-day. I wanted to tell you all my troubles, and you talk to me as though I were a professor."

"I didn't mean to be unkind," said I. "If you are really serious, I'm sorry."

"Sorry, why sorry?" he asked, quickly.

"It's such an old story. You fall in love with a girl's beautiful face—it's not the first time you've done it. You endow her with all sorts of qualities; you make her into an idol; and the whole thing only means that your aesthetic sense is gratified. That's a poor way of loving."

"It's a very real way," said Gerald, with some warmth. "I think you are horribly unsympathetic."

"I am in earnest," I answered. "A very short while ago you were quite taken up with Bella Sturgis. You don't care the least for her feelings; you simply follow your impulses, and desert her for a more attractive woman."

I do not know what made me espouse Bella's cause; perhaps I was hurt, more than I had time to realize, and seized on the first weapon to my hand.

"You don't spare *my* feelings," Gerald said, in a low voice. "All I can say is, that if Mary Hatherley won't have anything to do with me, I shall go away; I shall go and shoot big game—anything to get out of this horrible place. I *am* in earnest. I wasn't in earnest about Bella. I admired her very much, and all that, and mother is always urging me to marry; I should probably have drifted into marrying her——" he broke off.

I felt an unreasoning anger against him.

"Poor Bella!" I cried. "You may drift into marrying her yet."

That finished our conversation. He went away without another word, leaving me alone with my anger and my heartache.

CHAPTER VII

I confess that about this time I was led astray and over-mastered by conflicting emotions. My work, and my battles with Lady Harman's peculiarities, became unutterably irksome. I forgot how to efface myself; I spoke at the wrong moment, and on the wrong subject. I did not remember to be sympathetic, and I expected sympathy; in fact, I confused what was permitted to Mary Hatherley with what was permitted to Mary Gower, with the result that I drank the cup of bitterness each day, the cup of triumph each night.

At this time I was much sought after; my devotion to art was supposed to denote genius, though it was hardly respectable, and wholly unnecessary; but people forgave me my persistent refusal to see anyone, or to go anywhere during the day, and asked me to their houses in the evening.

I was often chaperoned by Lady Harman, sometimes by Dr. Trefusis himself. I had many admirers, but I only remember them vaguely, like figures in a dream. The golden key that opened their hearts led me into strange places; some had never really been tenanted, and were so cold and bare that I felt they could never really be warm or pleasant; others had been swept and garnished, and I was asked to believe that all traces of their former occupants were gone; others were full of rust and cobwebs, and old toys broken and thrust away; there was no room even for a new plaything. The key unlocked no sanctuary, with altar-lights and incense burning, waiting for the one divinity that was to fill its empty shrine. Those who loved me had loved before, and would love again.[20]

Women, whose idol is success, worshipped me too, in their curious fashion; it became desirable in their eyes to be known as the friend of Mary Hatherley; a note of distinction was thus sounded. They were proud to demonstrate the fact that they were above jealousy, or fear of rivalry.

I liked many of them, with a liking tempered by amusement. I am glad to think now that I did not interfere wantonly with their lovers, their husbands, or their sons. I was discreet, to the verge of being disagreeable: indeed, had it not been for my face, I think they might almost have resented my indifference· to their male belongings, and taken it as a personal affront.

I saw a great deal of Gerald, in the character of Mary Hatherley: the frost held, and he remained in London without a murmur; he was not much at home during the day; and Mary Gower had no speech with him alone.

"Something has happened to Gerald," Betty said one day. "I mean besides this business about Mary." They called her Mary by this time. "He wanders about picture galleries, I've found out; and some one saw him the other day in the British Museum. Isn't that somewhere in the city?"

"Not quite so bad," said I. The city had been Betty's terror, ever since she had been taken to the Tower as a child. "But isn't Mr. Harman merely improving his mind?"[21]

"Yes, but why?" cried his sister. "He's done very well all these years without it. It isn't as though he were the sort of man who could do nothing else. He can ride and shoot better than any man I know. Why should he want to improve his mind?"

Her somewhat incoherent speech amused me; and it was true. A superficial culture would have sat oddly on Gerald Harman, whose charm lay in his simplicity and a certain gallant bearing that might have fitted him to be the hero of a romance of the Elizabethan age, in which men were either knights or shepherds, full of a natural bravery, and keenly susceptible to the influence of women's beauty.

"Miss Hatherley is an artist," I suggested, in answer to Betty's remarks. She shrugged her shoulders.

"Mary Hatherley's just flirting with him," said she.

This was true: I had answered his letter, not in writing, nor indeed by any explicit word of mouth; but I had been kind, and had let him see that the letter had not displeased me; I had also led him to understand that the time was not yet come for any more open speech on his part. I was capricious: I used my power with but little mercy: these were days when I made him miserable; and days when I knew the world was re-created for him by my kindness.

Yet I was more wretched than I had ever been when I was only
Mary Gower. I grew to hate the other Mary's beautiful face; her
smile; the gracious turn of her head; her shapely hands. I grew
to hate all this with a passionate intensity that frightened me.[22] I
seemed to have realized Mary Hatherley in a strange, objective
way, as distinct from myself. She was the woman Gerald Harman
loved; she was the woman I should have been, and was not; and
then came a heart-stricken moment when I knew she was the
woman who had done both Gerald and another a wrong that
might never be undone.

It happened in this wise. I had gone down one day to the girls'
sitting-room to fetch a book I had left there, when I met Gerald
on the stairs. He passed me by with the briefest possible word,
and with a look of annoyance on his face that I was at a loss to
account for, till I reached the sitting-room, and found Bella Sturgis there.

She was sitting with her face on her arms, by the writing-table,
and I could see that she was crying. My instinct was to leave her;
but I was not quick enough to escape her notice, and she turned
upon me with an angry movement.

"Why didn't you knock?" said she.

In her confusion and distress she mistook me for a servant.
I should have laughed, had I not been overcome by the conviction that Gerald had just left her; and that something had passed
between them, which was connected with Mary Hatherley.

"I am sorry if I disturbed you," said I. "I have come for a book
I left here."

Then she saw her mistake, and flushed red.

"I beg your pardon; I really didn't see—" she said; and then,
as though bowed down by the weight of her own distress, she
dropped her head again on her hands.

I did not know what to do. It seemed an intrusion to remain;
and impossible to go.

"Forgive me," I said, at last. "You are in some trouble. I have
intruded upon you unknowingly; I can't go away without saying I
wish I could do something for you."

She looked up at me, with manifest surprise; tears shone still upon her face, and in her eyes. I wondered that Gerald had left her, even for Mary Hatherley.

"Why should you care?" she asked.

"I'm always sorry for another woman," I said.

She looked at me again, with a miserable, uncertain air; her haughty self-confidence had gone from her, and I felt emboldened to speak again.

"You may not know that I am Lady Harman's secretary. I have been in the house all day for a long while; and I can't help seeing a great deal of what goes on in it. I know your trouble, Miss Sturgis."

She got up at that, and looked for a moment as though she would have struck me; then she suddenly lost her self-control, and burst into tears. Those tears were dreadful to me: I took her hand, and soothed her as though she had been a child, and presently she sat down beside me.

"How do you know?" she said. "You can't know."

"I've heard them talk of Mary Hatherley," said I.

"And I suppose they say I'm breaking my heart?" cried she, with a desperate attempt at scorn.

"They would not be far wrong," I answered.

She gave a long sigh.

"It hurts," she said, quite simply.

Shame and an aching remorse seized me. I had taken him from her; and had roused in him a love which must be always barren. I had surely put a knife into Bella's heart; and her simple words stabbed me back. Did I not know it hurt! I carried the self-same wound.

"Do you care for him so much?" I said.

At first she would not answer, and frowned, while the tears came into her eyes; then she said, brokenly, "Yes—but we used to quarrel, and now it's all over."

"Do you think," I went on, "that if Mary Hatherley were to go away you could win him back?"

She pondered. I watched her beautiful face, and thought that I had hitherto misjudged her: her pride, the insolence of her beauty, her caprices, had been but the superficial manifestation of a passionate spirit, led astray by a world which cared only for the outer woman. Now that these things had been flung back in her face, her heart spoke: she lost the sense of her beauty, and its rights, and was more lovely than she had ever been—and did not know it.

"He used to love me, I'm sure," she said. "I believe he would again—I would not be so unkind—Oh, but what's the use of talking!"

I hardly heard the sound of my own voice as I answered her; there was a singing in my ears.

"I think he has been led away by a pretty face. I daresay he does not care for the real Mary Hatherley. He may return; be kind to him when he does."

"Oh, I will, I will," said she. "You have made me feel happier— I was so unhappy."

She bent forward impulsively, and kissed me. I kissed her back. "I am so glad," I said, and left the room hurriedly, to hide my emotion.

On my way home I went to see Dr. Trefusis. I found him alone, sitting over a pile of great folio volumes. His study, where I had so often found a refuge from the ills of life, looked warm and cheerful, with its shelves of books from floor to ceiling, and great, open hearth. He appeared to rouse himself with some difficulty, and I noticed he looked older, and very wearied.

"I'm not come to disturb you," said I. "Let me sit by the fire whilst you read. I have something I want to think out."

"It will do me good to talk, child," he answered. "I've been poring over these books for too long. What is it you have to think over, Mary?"

"Only the old thing."

He looked at me with a quickened attention.

"I've been thinking over it too," he said.

Then he sat down on the other side of the fireplace. The room was aglow with the flames, and the bright light of two lamps; there seemed also to be a strange light on Dr. Trefusis' face.

"You know, Mary," he began solemnly, "that this case of yours has led me into strange studies, and strange speculations. They are all wicked; I am going to put away my books, for I begin to fear lest they should take me into places where madness lies, outside the phenomenal, where we were never meant to penetrate. You have shown me how human longing, if it be powerful enough, is nearly omnipotent, for evil as well as for good. Here, in these old books, in the *Magia Naturalis* of Johannes Faust, in this old Latin of Cornelius Agrippa, and many others, I learn how spirits 'can be dragged out of the air'; how alchemy can turn metal to gold.[23] These things have a terrible fascination; but it is of the devil. I shall put them all away. Your longing turned Mary Gower, whom God made, into Mary Hatherley in whom He has no part."

He looked at me, with a shudder.

"The church put the alchemists to death for a less sin," he said. "This power you have brings you nothing but trouble: it may bring trouble to those you do not wish to injure. Mary, I implore you to stop, before it is too late."

All this in the mouth of Dr. Trefusis—the keen scientist, the ardent advocate of materialism—surprised me much. The gravity of his tone, so far removed from his ordinary carelessness, carried authority. All he said was my own inward, but unformulated, conviction put into words.

I asked him why he thought it might bring trouble to others.

"I have seen enough," he answered, "to understand your relations with the Harmans. It won't do, Mary. That young Harman ought not to be sacrificed to your love of experimentalizing."

At that I got up, and walked about the room.

"You do me injustice," said I. "I may have given way to a curiosity which, taken alone, would not be legitimate, but my heart was concerned in this matter."

"Ah," said he. "I feared so."

I sat down on a stool at his feet, and gave him all my confidence. He did not interrupt me; and when I had finished, we were both silent for a long while.

"Do you not feel yourself, that such a state of things cannot go on?" he said, at last.

"I am determined to give it up," I answered. "To-morrow night shall be Mary Hatherley's last appearance."

"Why let her appear again at all?" he asked.

"Because I'm a woman: and I want to say good-bye to Gerald Harman."

The doctor laughed; I think to cover some emotion.

"Well, well, well," he said. "Have it so if you will. But be done with the thing. It's unholy: it's a work of the devil. There are more things in heaven and earth than ever I dreamt of in my philosophy; things I dare not tamper with.[24] Now, Mary, will you climb to the top of the ladder, and put away Faustus, and Agrippa, and the rest? I've had enough of them."

We spent some time putting away the books—strange volumes; full of odd, symbolical drawings, and with wonderful titles, such as "The Golden Tripod"; "The Glory of the World, or the Gate of Paradise"; "The All-Wise Doorkeeper."[25]

The doctor crossed himself, as I put the last one in its place; and I laughed, in spite of my trouble.

"I've one thing more to say," he cried, turning suddenly on me. "I'm getting old, Mary, and I want a housekeeper, and a daughter. You refused me these once; you shall not refuse again. You and Miss Whateley must come and take charge of me. I promise you I'll age rapidly, and then you'll feel you are fulfilling a duty—a sensation dear to the soul of woman, I know."

We sat there over the fire for another hour. Before I left him, my promise had been given.

CHAPTER VIII

I woke the next morning with something of that indifference to life, which is the secret of so many peaceful deaths.

Mary Hatherley was condemned; she had but a brief hour left, and I knew not how she was to spend it. I only knew that she had to bid good-bye to Gerald Harman. The present hung before me like a veil; I could see the dim future moving behind it, a spectral army of figures all in gray; but they marched, this colourless procession of the years, with a monotony that grew into peace.

The thought of Mary Hatherley hardly troubled me. I did not care; I had passed through many deaths since that night when she had been born in all her beauty; for is not "every step we take in life a death in the imagination"?[26] I had held Beauty's sceptre, and had seen men slaves beneath it. I knew the isolation, the penalty of this greatness. Yet I owned that it was an empire for which it might well be worth paying. I held no theories based on mere sentiment; I owned that beauty might not possess all things; yet the woman who has not beauty neither has, nor pays. To this philosophy, or cynicism, I know not which to call it, had Mary Hatherley's experiences brought me.

I spent a strange day at Lady Harman's; the familiar place seemed unreal. In a week or two I should be gone, and all my days there would fade into the past; for I knew that I had no real hold on the lives of any of them, having come only as it were by accident into their midst, when they had treated me with as much kindness as was consistent with their education, their traditions, and the world in which they lived. Betty would marry one of her many lovers; and Clara someone who fed her intellectual vanity. And Gerald? I held my heart in check at the thought of Gerald.

I had met him first, as Mary Hatherley, in a crowd. It seemed like the logic of fate that I should take leave of him in a crowd; for our relations belonged to no world of peace and quietness, but to an order of life where Beauty, with her attendant pomp and circumstance, moved to the sound of music, and under the glare of a revealing light.

That evening we did not dance. There was singing, and stringed instruments; we moved about white stately rooms, where the music followed us like a memory. I spoke to many people, and knew nothing of what I said: at my heart was torture, in my soul peace. The rest of the world was blotted out when I saw Gerald coming to me.

At first he spoke but little; he had the desperate air of a man who is determined to know his fate—and his silence was charged with suggestion. We stood for a long while near the musicians, and the aching sweetness of one of Schubert's melodies pierced me with the sword of pain and pleasure wherewith music wounds her lovers. The whole measure of my grief seemed contained in that searching, divine air; in the human, passionate note of the strings; in the purer, more radiant tone of the flutes and hautboys.

Then Gerald looked into my eyes, and said, "Let us come away"; and I went blindly with him through the rooms, till we reached a door that opened into a garden.

The night was hardly cold, and very still; only a faint throbbing from the far-away streets lay at the heart of the silence, and troubled it. I could see the outline of Gerald's face in the starlight. He said nothing, but took me suddenly in his arms and kissed me; and in that moment I tasted the essence of life. Then he let me go. "Now send me from you if you can—if you dare," said he.

" 'Tis I who am going," I said.

"I am in earnest," answered he, "and I must have your answer."

"Oh, my answer," I cried, "is easily given. I do not love you. I can add something to that which you will not acknowledge. You have never loved me; you loved my face, but of my heart and soul you have known nothing."

I had not meant to say such words to him. I had meant to let him go with something like a benediction, but my bitterness rose up and made me speak.

"It is true I love your face," he said, quite gently. "But more than that. Why are you so unkind to me?"

Then there came a wild moment in which I was near telling

him all; and asking him if he could not love the soul of me, and take no thought for my body: but I paused, and remembered I had resolved never to let him know.

"I am not as unkind as I seem," I said. "It is kinder to tell you the truth. I am not made for love, or to be happy, and have children. I must live apart: do not ask me why; I cannot tell you. I shall not forget you; I hope you will forget me—at least, think of me without pain. And now, good-bye." I moved away.

"Is this your last word? Are you going to leave me so?" he cried out.

I stopped then, and looked back at him: the notes of a violin came through the silence like a shaft, and struck at my heart; they mingled with a woman's voice, in a love-song. I went to his side.

"I have one last word to leave you," I said to him. "You will forget me. When I am only a memory, go back to Bella; for you loved her."

He said nothing, and I was glad of the darkness, which covered my face. I turned back into the house, leaving him standing there; and went away, bidding no farewells.

I sat through that long night, and waited for the dawn; and when the dawn came, I kissed the wonderful reflected face of Mary Hatherley, and wished her a long good-bye.

"O face of my dreams," I said, "it is well that you should go back into nothingness; your hour is over; each moment held a possible joy; a surer pain: a brief triumph; a long regret. Let me decline into the lesser ways of life, where Beauty's flying feet have never passed; but where Peace may be seen stealing, a shadowy figure, with eyes looking towards the sun."[29]

NOTES

1   Olivia Shakespear never had the experience herself of sitting down and looking into a mirror at her "own unsatisfactory face"—she was a very beautiful woman. Her portrait on the cover of this book shows what she looked like when *Beauty's Hour* was written. Yeats kept this photograph for at least the next thirty years, writing to her in December 1926, "I came upon two early photographs of you yesterday, while going through my file—one that from Literary Year Book. Who ever had a like profile? a profile from a Sicilian coin. One looks back to one's youth as to [a] cup that a mad man dying of thirst left half tasted. I wonder if you feel like that." Allan Wade, ed., *The Letters of W. B. Yeats* (London: Rupert Hart-Davis, 1954) 721.

2   Bella Sturgis shares both her beautiful name, and her pride, among other attributes, with Bella Wilfer of *Our Mutual Friend*, constantly "pouting," with "a handful of brown curls in her mouth[.]" Charles Dickens, *Our Mutual Friend* (1865; Harmondsworth: Penguin, 1997) 44-45. Miss Sturgis is also very much kin to Blanche Ingram, Rochester's alleged beloved in *Jane Eyre* (1847), proud and beautiful and never noticing the poor governess in the same room.

3   Plain women, and their unhappiness with that plainness, are commonplace in 19th-century English fiction as never before nor since—particularly when the female character in question is narrating her own story, and when there is anything like a rival on the scene. Chiefest among them is plain Jane Eyre, who mourns, upon her arrival at Thornfield Hall, the "misfortune that I was so little, so pale, and had features so irregular and so marked." Charlotte Bronte, *Jane Eyre* (1847; Oxford: Clarendon, 1969) 119. Marian Halcombe is, like Jane and Mary, an unattractive woman with a brilliant mind and a way with words; that "the dark down on her upper lip [is] almost a moustache" and that she has "a large, firm, masculine mouth and jaw; prominent, piercing, resolute brown eyes; and thick, coal-black hair, growing unusually low down on her forehead" sets her quite apart from the pale, pretty, aptly named Fairlies. Wilkie Collins, *The Woman in White* (1860/1; Harmondsworth: Penguin, 1999) 35.

4   Mary Gower sounds, and looks, like Mary Garth. However,
         Mary Garth is a character created by a famously plain woman
         who wrote her novels under a man's name. And plain, patient,
         kind Mary Garth is rewarded—if that is the proper word—
         for her dedication to a handsome, frivolous man by marriage
         to him. George Eliot, *Middlemarch* (1871; Harmondsworth:
         Penguin, 1994).

5   The instance of a former governess offering her charge a home
         is rare. Jane Eyre intends it, but swiftly gets herself out of
         same: "I found the rules of the establishment were too strict,
         its course of study too severe for a child of her age: I took her
         home with me. I meant to become her governess once more,
         but I soon found this impracticable; my time and cares were
         now required by another— my husband needed them all. So
         I sought out a school conducted on a more indulgent system,
         and near enough to permit of my visiting her often, and
         bringing her home sometimes." *Jane Eyre* 363.

6   Compare the intense, immense, drug-induced pain turning
         Dr. Jekyll into Mr. Hyde, and back again, from "Henry Jekyll's
         Statement of the Case:"

         The most racking pangs succeeded: a grinding in the bones,
         deadly nausea, and a horror of the spirit that cannot be
         exceeded at the hour of birth or death. Then these agonies
         began swiftly to subside, and I came to myself as if out of a
         great sickness. Robert Louis Stevenson, *The Strange Case of Dr
         Jekyll and Mr Hyde and Other Stories* (1886; Harmondsworth:
         Penguin, 1979) 83.

         Mary's transformation needs no drugs, and does not hurt. It
         is a self-willed transformation before a mirror—a mirror that
         functions a bit like the Lady of Shalott's, and a bit like Alice's
         window into Wonderland. The desire is for beauty, not moral
         liberty past the point of humanity. In that, Shakespear owes a
         debt to Oscar Wilde and *The Picture of Dorian Gray* (1890/1).
         Initially, Basil Hallward paints Dorian Gray to preserve his
         great beauty for all time; however, Shakespear does not permit
         her heroine, once beauty is hers, to be a bad actor. When Mary
         Gower realizes the pain Mary Hatherley is causing—and Miss
         Hatherley has done nothing fatal, nor even criminal—Mary
         Hatherley disappears.

7   Shakespear's use of "personality" here as synonymous with

the physical "person" is interesting. Mary's narrative makes it quite clear that, beneath the lovely new skin, she's the same old Mary Gower—there is no change in her inward personality. I believe Shakespear is taking the equating of the two, along with much more, from Oscar Wilde. In both *Dorian Gray* and *The Importance of Being Earnest*, Wilde used the words interchangeably, and particularly when talking about beauty. It was a gloss of sorts, to excuse his male characters' speaking of a beautiful man: loving, even worshipping, a beautiful personality wouldn't get you into trouble, but loving a beautiful person would. In defending Basil Hallward's passion for Dorian Gray, and his own letters to Lord Alfred Douglas, at his trials for "gross indecency" in the spring of 1895, Wilde had tried to make this argument in his own defense. The passage was reported in the contemporary police gazettes, and known to those who had attended the trial—or who, like Yeats, had supported the Wilde family by calling on Lady Wilde in London and discussing it among themselves in private letters, and, one may assume, in person. When Edward Carson asked him if Hallward's "idolatry" for Dorian "describes a natural feeling of one man towards another," Wilde would only reply that it "describes the influence produced on an artist by a beautiful personality," and flatly refused to be led to speak of a beautiful "person." The jury didn't buy it—any more than we think, here, that Mary Gower would be delighted by a new inside (she rather likes hers as is) rather than a new, gorgeous outside. See Merlin Holland, ed., *The Real Trial of Oscar Wilde* (New York: HarperCollins, 2003) 85-86; 89.

8   Though it takes drugs to change Jekyll into Hyde, and back again, Hyde flourishes at night. Dracula, revitalized by Bram Stoker the year after Shakespear's story appeared in *The Savoy*, but written about for centuries in folk tales and in John Polidori's *The Vampyre* (1819), is of course a creature of the night. Similarly and less horribly, the folk- and fairy-tale heroine Cinderella loses her various glamors and enhancements at the stroke of midnight. From 1697, Charles Perrault's version had added the fairy godmother and other enchanting elements to the old Cinderella tale; available also to Shakespear would have been the Brothers Grimm's version of Aschenputtel, published in the early 1800s, and Margaret Hunt's two-volume English translation of 1884. *Beauty's Hour* is very much a Cinderella story, but without a princess ending for Mary Gower.

9   The mention of 18th and early 19th century English portraitist
         George Romney and his untouchable faces—Romney is still
         most famous for his beautiful women, chiefly his paintings
         of Horatio Nelson's beloved, Lady Emma Hamilton—shows
         that Mary Gower knows something about art, enough to style
         Mary Hatherley as a painter.

10   Like Cinderella, Mary Hatherley makes her public debut at a
         ball; and, also, her last appearance.

11   This paragraph contains almost verbatim the suggestions Yeats
         had about Gerald's character and changes Shakespear should
         make. Writing to her in August of 1894, Yeats mentioned he
         knew she was "getting near the end" of writing her novella,
         and, in a fascinating passage that also amplifies his idea of
         masks—and uncannily presages the character of Gerald
         Ashburnham in Ford Madox Ford's novel *The Good Soldier* (1915)
         —Yeats suggested that "Gerald wants a slight touch more of
         definition. A few lines early in the book would do all needed.
         You find he develops into rather a plastic person; and this is
         the best thing for the plot, but you should show that this is
         characterization & not a limitation of knowledge. Might he not
         be one of those vigerous fair haired, boating or cricket playing
         young men, who are very positive, & what is called manly,
         in external activities & wholly plastic & passive in emotional
         & intellectual things? I met just such a man last winter. I had
         suspected before that those robust masks hid often and often
         a great emotional passivity and plasticity but this man star-
         tled me. He was of the type of those who face the cannons
         mouth without a tremour, but kill themselves rather than face
         life without some girl with pink cheaks, whose character they
         have never understood, whose soul they have never perceived,
         & whom they would have forgotten in a couple of months.
         Such people are very lovable for both their weakness & their
         strength appear pathetic; and your clever heroine night well
         love him. She would see how strong & courageous he was in
         the external things, where a woman was weak, & would feal
         instinctively how much in need of protection & care in those
         deeper things where she was strong." W. B. Yeats, *The Collected
         Letters of W. B. Yeats*, ed. John Kelly and Eric Domville, Volume
         I (Oxford: Clarendon, 1986) 396.

12   Billingsgate was the area of London best known for its fish
         market. Mrs Harman's concern for the poor close to home,
         and, more comfortably for her, in faraway lands—while rather

blithely ignoring the proceedings and problems of her own family—is very like that of Mrs. Jellyby, whose "African project" of "cultivating coffee and educating the natives of Borrioboola-Gha, on the left bank of the Niger," occupies her entirely as her children go unfed and tumble down flights of stairs. Charles Dickens, *Bleak House* (1853; New York: Everyman, 1907) 34.

13 This weariness with traditional English beef and mutton is unsurprising if poor Mary must eat some every day to show her appreciation, but Shakespear may also be making a gentle joke at her lover's vegetarianism. Yeats was from 1889 into the 1890s a vegetarian, partly because of his increasing belief in reincarnation, and partly because he had no money and vegetables were cheaper than meat. His friend Katharine Tynan recalled with a shudder her supper with Yeats "at a vegetarian restaurant somewhere about Charing Cross . . . There was a long and elaborate menu, but after the first or second course I felt that never again, as long as I lived, could I have any appetite, so Willie had the rest of the meal, my portions as well as his own." Katharine Tynan, *Twenty-Five Years: Reminiscences* (New York: Devin-Adair, 1913) 281.

14 In many versions of the Cinderella story, including the popular film *Ever After* (1998), Cinderella takes her mother's name as a very thin disguise. Mary's choice of her mother's name reminds us that, like so many other Victorian heroines, she is an orphan; arguably she has a father figure in Dr. Trefusis, but none for a mother. That Hatherley sounds like Hathaway, the maiden name of the wife of the most famous English writer named Shakespear(e), is an amusing move on Shakespear's part.

15 The monster in Mary Shelley's *Frankenstein* (1818) manages to explain this, with the help of having read John Milton.

16 Mr. Hyde's recklessness takes the form of murder and mayhem. Mary's takes the form of shopping at night, and going to the theater. That these everyday prerogatives for a man—simply walking the London streets and amusing himself—can be adventuresome and challenging for even a privileged woman is a strong reminder that there are only male *flâneurs*. A woman walking the streets at night is still too strongly associated with one word only in 1896: streetwalker.

17 The square where Dr. Trefusis lives is here identified as Dorchester Square. Shakespear's own home at the time was in Portchester Square.

18 In *The Picture of Dorian Gray*, Sibyl Vane initially mesmerizes

Dorian as Juliet, with her "little flower-like face," "small Greek
head" and voice with "all the tremulous ecstasy that one hears
just before dawn when the nightingales are singing" (DG
44-45). She loses him, and consequently takes her own life as
Juliet does, playing the same role after she has fallen in love
with him, when the reality of love lets her see "through the
hollowness, the sham, the silliness of the empty pageant" (DG
69). Mary Gower is performing a role as Mary Hatherley—
and here she senses, as she looks at Gerald, the jeopardies of
continuing to play the role, or of stepping out of it. Shakespear,
like Wilde, clearly loves Shakespeare.

19   Christian Rosenkrantz, who may or may not have lived in the
1400s and who was the inspiration for the Rosicrucian sect,
and Pope Honorius I, denounced as a heretic in 680 AD, were
mystical as well as religious figures. Yeats was a member of the
inner Order of the Golden Dawn, which was Rosicrucian; he
had been initiated into this inner Order in January 1893. The
material which Shakespear uses here evidently came from
Yeats, along with her use of the Grimoire of Pope Honorius.

20   In Yeats's poem of 1899, "Aedh Laments the Loss of Love"
("The Lover Mourns for the Loss of Love"), Yeats uses very
similar language and ideas in speaking of Shakespear's unhappiness at finding such a "former occupant," Maud Gonne, still
in his heart. W. B. Yeats, *The Wind Among the Reeds* (London:
Elkin Mathews, 1903) 21.

21   Gerald's attempt to render himself an artistic aesthete for
Mary Hatherley's sake is clearly doomed to fail, and rather like
Archibald Grosvenor's similar ploy to get the girl in Gilbert &
Sullivan's *Patience* (1881). Grosvenor pretends to be a "greenery-
yallery, Grosvenor Gallery, foot-in-the-grave" aesthetic poet,
modeled on Oscar Wilde, but wins Patience, in the end, as
himself: "steady and stolidly, jolly Bank-Holiday everyday
young man." W. S. Gilbert and Arthur Sullivan, *Patience; or,
Bunthorne's Bride* (London: Chappell, 1881) 37.

22   The phrase "passionate intensity" is worth noting as a particular. Whether Shakespear's own, or supplied by Yeats as he
read and edited her story (though he does not mention this line
in his surviving letters), it is a phrase entirely associated with
him today. The first stanza of *The Second Coming* (1919), one of
Yeats's best-known and most quoted poems, ends with: "The
best lack all conviction, while the worst / Are full of passionate
intensity."

23   Johann Faust, 16th-century German alchemist, is better known
       today in his fictional manifestations as the scientist who sells
       his soul to the devil in Christopher Marlowe's *Doctor Faustus*
       (1604?) and Johann Wolfgang von Goethe's *Faust* (begun 1806).
       Faust's contemporary Heinrich Cornelius Agrippa was a theo-
       logian, alchemist, and scholar of the occult.

24   "There are more things in heaven and earth, Horatio, than are
       dreamt of in your philosophy." William Shakespeare, *Hamlet*
       (1599-1602?), I.v.167-8.

25   In 1893, Arthur Edmund Waite published in London the first
       English translation of *The Hermetic Museum*. From the Latin
       original, published in Frankfurt in 1678, this massive anthology
       contains "twenty-two most celebrated Chemical Tracts"
       including the most elusive and important one, "instructing
       all disciples of the Sopho-Spagyric Art how that greatest and
       truest medicine of The Philosopher's Stone may be found and
       held." The search for the stone that could turn base metals to
       gold, among other things, has obsessed centuries of human
       history and continues as a fascination today; witness J. K.
       Rowling choosing to make the safekeeping of the Philosopher's
       Stone (or, as it was translated for an American readership, the
       Sorcerer's Stone) main plot focus of her first Harry Potter
       novel. *The Golden Tripod*, *The Glory of the World*, and *The All-
       Wise Doorkeeper*, the last being a series of ten alchemical draw-
       ings following the Book of Genesis from Chaos through the
       creation of Adam and Eve, were all included in *The Hermetic
       Museum*.

26   W. B. Yeats (as "Ganconagh"), *John Sherman & Dhoya* (London:
       Fisher Unwin, 1891; Lilliput, 1990) 31.

27   Compare the ending of the first chapter of Yeats, *John Sherman*
       (9): "'Go yonder, to those other joys and other sceneries I have
       told you of.' It bade him who loved still stay and dream, and
       gave flying feet to him who imagined."